BECAUSE YOU'RE MINE

MARIN MONTGOMERY

COPYRIGHT

COVER DESIGN: LOUISA MAGGIO
EDITING: BOOKTIQUE EDITING

DESCRIPTION

When Levin Crowdley stumbles upon evidence that suggests her adoring fiancé is behind the murder of her childhood best friend, she knows fleeing from him is the only way to stay alive.

But Alec won't be left that easily.

In fact, nobody has ever left him and lived to tell.

The moment Alec finds their dream home empty and Levin's engagement ring lying in the crib he'd purchased for the baby he intended to have with her, he knows she's gone, and she knows something.

And so he does what he has to do.

He pursues her.

He hunts her down like a dog chasing a rabbit.

And the second he catches her, he's *never* letting go.

'Til death do them part.

This book is dedicated to my childhood friend, now my mentor, who has been with me through every significant passage in my life. The comfort of having a friend who has watched you grow in life, both in age and in enlightenment, is a rare find.

"Toodles," thanks for being a lifelong friend.

CHAPTER ONE

LEVIN

I'M LEAVING TODAY, BUT I SHOULD'VE LEFT YESTERDAY.

My bags are packed and loaded haphazardly in the backseat and trunk of my rental car which is parked down the street.

I'm sitting on my bed wringing my hands in nervous anticipation as the shower spews water from the bathroom, then slows to a trickle as it shuts off.

My plan to leave him is complicated, not unlike my fiancé. He isn't good at letting people go.

The diamond on my ring finger feels heavy—almost as weighted as his proposal.

The reason for leaving is decidedly divergent from why most people leave their significant other. There's no cheating that I know about. He didn't physically hit me. Yet, his abuse is the worst form—slow and painful.

It crept up on me little by little—snide comments that

got under my skin or a suggestion here and there that wasn't a suggestion but a loaded recommendation.

According to him, my ass could be rounder or my stomach could be flatter. He doesn't call me 'fat,' he just plants the seed that I can use improvement.

So, he hired me a personal trainer.

He wants my hair longer. It's not growing fast enough. He insists on extensions. The copper-colored, chin-length hair is now past my shoulders.

The *Target* and *Old Navy* brand clothing I used to wear, he throws out. For the masses, he says I need to be 'unique.' My clothes are selected by him. He says my wardrobe is a reflection of him.

Boobs? He wants them bigger. He's always pointing out women who have boobs he considers the 'perfect' size. I put my foot down and refuse to get plastic surgery. He pushes but finally recants... because now he wants a baby.

That isn't the worst part. All of this is superficial.

I discovered he was involved in my best friend's murder.

Each minute with Alec is torture. My nights are a restless combination of tossing and turning and staring at the clock, the red numbers a reminder of each passing minute I'm under his thumb.

When he looks at me, my heart palpitations seem to boom like a loudspeaker announcing my intentions to leave. Does he know I know? How much longer can I pretend before this secret eats me alive, and I put my own life at risk?

Eric's will had put me in a tailspin. He cut Alec out entirely. I'm the sole beneficiary, only my spouse and children will have access to the money.

It's made me question if Alec loves me or is looking for deep pockets.

I'm impatient as I wait for him to get out of the shower and finish grooming his body.

If you asked him, he would tell you in no uncertain terms that he's a work of art with a gorgeous topography. Alec's jet-black hair matches his eyes, and some would argue his soul.

I was scared to live with him, yet more terrified to leave him.

Until today.

All I could think about was Eric McGrath, my childhood best friend and Alec's business partner, who suddenly passed a year ago. The police said suicide. Eric was found hanging in his bedroom closet, his belt wrapped around his neck. That story hadn't seemed plausible. Eric hadn't seemed depressed when I had spoken to him a few days before his death.

It wasn't until Eric's death that I met Alec in person at his funeral. If you ask me, a great place to meet your soulmate! Eric and Alec had been business partners in a real estate development company.

I shake my head in disgust as I think back to the funeral, and the way Alec had sat and stared at the closed casket, a look of pretend disbelief on his face. The pure evil of him as he sat with Eric's parents and looked devastated, thick tears sliding down his cheeks.

Eric's parents introduced me to Alec, crumpled tissues in hand. Alec and I had crossed paths once or twice via *FaceTime* or when I called Eric's office to chat, but I had moved overseas to Europe to do some backpacking and soul-searching and had been a virtual stranger for the year before his death.

But now, the only stranger in the house is Alec Durant, my fiancé.

CHAPTER TWO

ALEC

IF I'M LATE FOR MY 8:00 A.M. APPOINTMENT WITH TAD Johnson, an investor from Utah, I'm blaming Levin. She had tossed and turned last night, and it had kept me awake. She must be anxious, as she's only restless when she has something on her mind. Whatever the issue, it would have to wait. I would ask her later after I took care of business.

With my morning shower and shave complete, I exit the bathroom and find Levin perched on the bed wringing her hands.

I glance at my Breitling and then at her. Weird. It's after 7:00 a.m. Typically, she works out with her trainer at 7:30 before heading to the animal shelter to save one more underprivileged beast from their demise.

The outfit was also off. She wasn't wearing workout clothes today. Her clothing choice is suspect—no sign of *Lululemon* athleisure wear. The new tan *Burberry* handbag and flowered *Alice + Olivia* dress were much too dressy for even a casual day at the office. Levin didn't work outside the home, so this was odd.

"What're you doing?" I ask.

Levin isn't paying attention to me. She's lost in her thoughts.

"Levin?" I snap my fingers.

She glances up shocked to see me standing in front of her. She swallows hard.

"What?" Her voice sounds small and far away even though I'm standing three inches from her face.

"I asked what you were doing." I give her a hard stare exhaling through my nose. "You're dressed like you're skipping the gym today." I reach down and grab her chin, "And I hope that isn't the case. I know how irritable you get when you miss a day of Barre."

Levin knows my strict requirements for any woman I date—especially my future bride. I require that she have a personal trainer and a nutritionist to prepare our meals.

Manicures, pedicures, and facials were a part of the lifestyle, and she never balked at the amount of time it took for her to learn how to apply her makeup just perfectly or have her hair blown out to my specifications.

The fact of the matter is I love spoiling and dressing her up like a doll. She has a desirable figure—B-cup tits and a small waist with long legs. I have no problem taking credit for the woman she's become. I also have no issue with improving upon her physique.

She's my trophy, my most prized possession. Due to my line of work, it's paramount that the woman on my arm reflects class and poise, and a certain, shall we say, richness. Exclusivity.

Exclusively mine, to be specific.

Her appearance must be custom-tailored to match my custom-made lifestyle.

"No gym this morning." She fakes a yawn. "I didn't sleep well last night."

"I could tell." I smooth down her long, shiny, brunette hair. "You kept me up in the process."

"Sorry," she mumbles, half-hearted, crossing and uncrossing her legs.

"Still doesn't explain why you're overdressed on a Monday."

"I'm going to go have breakfast with a potential client." Her voice is stilted.

"I thought we already discussed you working outside the house." I pinch her cheek. "We decided no."

"*You* decided that." She rolls her eyes at me. "It doesn't matter, it's just a meeting."

I didn't like her tone, but I had to let it go. I gave her a warning look and stepped back. My meeting with some potential clients had me sidetracked, and that's my priority this morning.

I couldn't wait for the kill.

"The thrill of the kill" had been my tagline since my earliest days in real estate. There was nothing that got me off more than closing deals.

And the right woman.

Levin's lying to me. I know it.

When someone lies to me, I love the art of catching them —the amusement as they trip over their words to try to find a new direction to take their dishonesty.

It isn't as fun with my fiancée, especially when it involves her lying to me.

However, this would have to wait until later.

I switch topics since the conversation of her having a job outside the home is ridiculous. There's no point in arguing it. I said no. My mind isn't changing.

I decide on a new tactic.

"Baby?" I change the tone in my voice.

"Hmm?" She looks bothered.

"I have a thing tonight, a dinner. Bradshaw's, 8:00 p.m. I need you there."

"Tonight?" She frowns. "But you know I volunteer at the animal shelter on Mondays."

Her and the damn animals of the world and her plans to save them all.

"You can't." It comes out brusque, more so than intended. "I'll have a driver pick you up at seven. If you have to volunteer, do it this morning, but change your outfit."

"Client names?" She sighs.

"Tone." I prod her. "This is what pays the bills and makes you look like a million bucks."

Her face softens. She stands up from the bed.

I cup her neck and kiss her—once on the cheek and once on the mouth. She recoils.

What the fuck is going on? This moping around the house has got to stop. She's got too much time on her hands. Time for the next progression in life.

"Yes, Al, I'll be there."

She knows calling me 'Al' is akin to calling me Alvin, my real name.

Levin is trying to annoy me, but I don't have the time or energy to engage, though the thought of rough sex crosses my mind.

I decide against it. There's nothing like mixing passion and anger for heated and carnal desire, but money calls.

"Baby, get to the gym." My hands circle her waist. "You need to release some tension..." I kiss her neck, "And don't worry, I'll release some for you later."

I slap her tight ass and walk out of the bedroom.

Still, something is off. It's not just her behavior that's alarming—she can be moody at times like all women.

I realize as I grab an apple from the fridge that there are hardly any groceries left. Most of yesterday was spent at work, but grocery shopping was done by Levin for our week ahead on Sundays.

Clearly, she didn't make it to the store. Our cook usually told her ahead of time what was needed for meal prep, and she would bring home the items for them to put together today.

That was odd.

I swipe my keys off the counter on my way out.

Heading into the garage, I notice a piece of our Louis Vuitton luggage is missing.

Weird.

Her Range Rover is unlocked. I check the backseat and trunk.

Nothing.

I didn't have any idea why she would put luggage in my vehicle, but I open the trunk of my A7 for confirmation.

Still nothing.

I start to turn around and head back inside when my cell phone shrills, my 8:00 a.m. client's name flashing across the screen.

Shit. I have to take this. The man is flying in from Utah to look at building a hospital on some prime real estate, and I stand to make a pretty penny if all goes well.

My pulse is pounding in my ear.

I hit the 'accept' button my phone, take a deep breath, and answer, a tension headache starting to build at the base of my neck.

Levin is up to something, and it's no good.

If she wanted a head start, she's going to get it.

CHAPTER THREE

Levin

I smooth my dress and hair as Alec walks out of the bedroom, my hands shaking. The garage door motor creaks as he and his silver Audi pull out into the street.

A month ago, he'd purchased me a candy-apple red Range Rover that was sitting on the other side of the garage. It would continue to sit there, just a reminder of me.

I didn't trust him. I didn't trust it didn't have a tracking device on it.

Alec would inadvertently mention details concerning my day that I hadn't shared with him. A pattern would start to materialize after I would talk on the phone with the few friends I stayed in touch with.

The guilty look would creep onto his face after he gave himself away, his lips pressed down hard as if he could keep the words from spewing out of his mouth.

Cameras had started to appear in various locations around the house. Video surveillance can be necessary in some places

—not in our bathroom or office. Privacy shrouded Alec's personal life, but my life with him is examined under a microscope aka his watchful eyes.

My Chevy Impala rental was parked two houses down in front of the Miller's, rented under the name of a close friend I'd met at the gym—one hell-bent on helping me escape Alec's clutches. Lucky for me, Alec had never met her, never even heard of her. She didn't travel in our circle. She didn't have fake tits, drive a Benz, or fashion herself an accessory on a rich man's arm. She was just a fellow gym-going mom with an approachable smile and a heart of gold—the kind of woman Alec would walk past and not think twice about.

Yesterday, I had filled the trunk of the Impala with necessities that Alec wouldn't notice—mainly toiletries and groceries.

As soon as I saw his vehicle drive past the house, I knew it was time to go.

My legs wobble. I need to get ahold of myself. I reach out and balance myself on the closet door.

I have to get away from my past and do so in record time.

I need as much distance as possible between us.

There was one perplexing question—did I leave the ring or take it?

It was a gorgeous, handcrafted diamond he had designed with his jeweler, but I also knew it cost a small fortune, and I might need the money.

The ring was as easy to part with as Alec, but it could buy me more time.

I decide that I will leave it lying in the crib.

He had insisted on the crib. In the nursery he demanded.

The room was tastefully decorated in gender-neutral colors, and every detail down to the handmade bassinet and the striped linens considered. A tan stuffed bear that weighs as much as me is propped in the corner, its beady eyes staring at me with regret, and more importantly, a potential video recording device. I yank the bear around, paranoid this is another one of Alec's sly attempts to watch me.

There wasn't time to go back down memory lane, but it all came crashing back to me as I twist off the ring, the brilliant four carats sparkling in the light from the window in the nursery.

The proposal had happened in Fiji when we were on vacation four months ago.

Usually, I can foresee the turn of events in relationships, but this was a new one, even for me.

It was unexpected to say the least. We had only been dating for about a year, and he proposed on the anniversary of Eric's death, which Alec planned on purpose as a tribute to our dear friend. Something good to come out of the bad.

I believed him at the time—thought it was sweet.

It isn't a memory I like to conjure up because it reminds me of happier times before I knew he had the potential to be a cold-blooded killer.

Our waiter at the resort restaurant had come up to our table at the end of the meal to check on us. He had asked me to grab the check off of his tray which I thought was weird.

There, lying on the bill for our seafood and cocktails, was a blue box with a white ribbon that could mean only one thing.

The waiter smiled as my stomach did somersaults, and my head got fuzzy.

Alec nodded at me to go ahead and remove it from the tray. I gingerly took the Tiffany's box and formed the biggest smile I have ever composed in my life.

As I looked to my right where Alec was seated, I saw him get down on one knee. I started to gag and had to force myself not to throw up the expensive sea bass that was now lodged in my throat. I wasn't prepared for this.

Internally, I knew I had to get my nerves together, or I would mess up this proposal. I needed to keep mine intact.

This was overwhelming to me but not unwelcome.

"Levin," Alec took my hands in his, "I know this has been a rough year, but in the toughest time of my life, you came along. You have been the best thing that could ever happen to me." He searches my face and continues, "You are smart, sexy, and have made a one-woman man out of me. I can't imagine spending my life with anyone else. Will you marry me?"

He took the box from my lap and proceeded to pull out one of the largest and brightest diamonds I have ever seen. Tears shone in his eyes as he slid a Marquis-cut sparkler on my ring finger attached to my shaking hand.

I started to cry knowing we had bonded over a tragedy that had blossomed into love.

I whispered the word 'yes' before saying it over and over with more conviction each time.

There was unease, though.

For every 'yes' coming from my lips, my stomach twisted threatening to release the contents of my queasy stomach.

"I love you so much." I grabbed him by the neck and kissed him with all the passion I could muster in front of a group of excited patrons and wait staff at the restaurant.

He had secured us the best view of the South Pacific Ocean and had made sure that the Maitre'd was recording the momentous event. He was detail-oriented and had spared no expense in making sure the proposal was charming and thoughtful.

"Baby," I cried into his arms. "I'm so excited to be your wife." He held me close as pictures were snapped, and a smile played across his lips.

"Thank you." He grabbed my chin kissing me hard on the mouth.

"For what?" I wiped a tear from my eye. At least in

pictures and on video, it would look like I genuinely cared about being his wife.

"For making an honest man out of me. I know I didn't always make it easy. I'm just glad you stuck with me as I sorted through my shit and got over..." His voice trailed off.

That was the one point he had made which I understood. How hard Eric's death had been to get through—I would never be over it.

Alec's head tilted, his gaze trained on me. "I just wish Eric was here with us to see how happy we are. How he brought us together."

Alec looked glum, a quiet sadness in his eyes, and at that moment, I started to cry real tears of unhappiness, and I covered them by burying my head in Alec's shoulder.

I tried to get ahold of my feelings. "I miss him more than you'll ever know. He meant so much to both of us."

I covered Alec's hand with my own, now sparkling with the diamond reflecting off the candlelight. "I know he's here looking down on us, so happy."

In Fiji after his proposal, the topic of children came screeching to a halt in front of me. He confided in me the last day that he wanted to be a father soon, and that our marriage was icing on the cake to seal the deal. We were lying in bed the next morning after the surprise proposal.

Alec had never professed he wanted kids. In fact, he was adamant when going out to dinner that we choose adult-only restaurants, and when I offered a night off to a new mom next door, Alec flat out refused to help babysit.

It was suspect.

I snap back to reality when I hear my phone ring. It is a burner phone, one I acquired at a local cell phone provider. It has a limited number of minutes and isn't as high-tech as my current model. There's no *Facebook*. No *Instagram*. No email. It is a simple flip phone reminiscent of my teenage years when a cell phone was a novelty. With this, I'm virtually untraceable.

I know it's Maddy, my new friend. The one who is helping me out of this mess.

I fling the ring into the crib.

He can have it.

CHAPTER FOUR

ALEC

I HEAD TO THE OFFICE, MY 8:00 A.M. CONFIRMED. I SIGH IN relief. I need this deal and the money.

Dinner tonight would give me even more opportunity to make up some of the money I had lost in unsavory investments. Real estate is a gamble, and some payouts are higher than others, but if Eric had been doing his part in our business, this wouldn't have happened. The deal was closing this afternoon, and the commission would be a chunk of money I desperately needed.

I turn up the classic rock station and blast some AC/DC. My window comes down, and I'm tapping my fingers on the steering wheel. This could turn out to be one of the best days in recent memory.

Or one of the worst.

My thoughts drift to Levin—her weird behavior today—the missing luggage.

I think back to our last couple of months.

Sure, we've had a couple of bumps in the road, but who doesn't?

I remember how I felt after she accepted my marriage proposal—the weight off my shoulders.

She said yes. I breathed a sigh of relief as we headed back to our hotel room.

She said yes. I breathed a sigh of relief as we flew back to San Diego.

She said yes. I breathed a sigh of relief as we got settled into my house, and I promised her we could start looking at a shared home. She hadn't wanted to live together until marriage, but I was persuasive, and she finally gave in.

She always did. Not because she was a pushover, but because she needed stability in her life. Her childhood was chaotic, but she had gone to college and excelled at everything she did.

Others might be envious of her beauty, but I knew it went deeper which made her a rare commodity. Levin believed in enrichment, and she was the one always interested in charitable events and volunteering her time.

Before I'd requested she stop working, she had been a successful graphic designer.

But now it seemed she was leaving me. And I wasn't happy about it. Because now I wanted her—all of her. She was the total package, and I knew it.

Her personality is warm and inviting. My clients took to her like a moth to a flame. She could hold their attention and better yet, involve herself in their discussions without sounding like an airhead. Levin had the personality when I met her, but I gave her the finesse. The *je ne sais quoi*.

I had been careless with her feelings and her heart at times, a selfishness that profoundly disappointed me as I thought about what I had put her through. She deserved better, but she got me instead. I did my best to make up for it by giving her a life that most could only dream about.

I fell hard for her. I tried to resist by chasing other women, more deals, money, and by shutting her out.

Levin went, but not without a fight. She had staying power. She was worth it. She knew it.

I did not want a repeat of the other girl I thought I loved in college.

I came crawling back to Levin—defeated—but with a sense of purpose because I had more information to make an educated decision. Eric had been the final straw.

Eric McGrath had been my business partner. Keyword—had been.

If only Eric hadn't been so hell-bent on running the business himself, on pushing me out.

I had blown through millions of our money, yes, but I prefer the word 'invested.'

He didn't understand building a business from the ground up, and the development that comes with it. He had been the financial backer with daddy's money. I had been the mover and shaker of the business, and he had been the silver-spooned brains. I wish he had seen it before it was too late.

I knew the guilt of his actions had led him to kill himself—at least that's what I told myself and others.

Levin had grown up with me. I had known about her as he constantly mentioned her. Every childhood memory he brought up seemed to have her in it.

My first impression had been that they were in a relationship at one time, now friendly exes. That was, however, until I realized he had a hard-on for men.

The first time I had caught him, he had been in the backseat of his SUV with a real estate investor of ours. Who knew that scouting office space would result in me finding the perfect location and him finding a love connection?

After that encounter, which I never mentioned and pretended I didn't see, I made it my mission to watch Eric like a hawk.

Personally, I could care less about Eric's sexual identity. I did have an issue when business mixed with pleasure and resulted in catastrophic outcomes.

That client had made it his mission in life to try to use his sexual relationship with Eric as his security blanket when it came to representation. He had expected favors and cut commissions because he had been in Eric's mouth. This made for some perilous expectations.

I was relieved that Eric and Levin hadn't had a relationship beyond the platonic. It made it easier for me to whittle my way into her life after the funeral. Honing my way into her life had been relatively simple. I had been the one to check on her, comfort her, share stories and commonalities about Eric. The relationship happened naturally and over time.

After I had seen his will, and after I knew what he was worth and what his worth meant, Levin was his priceless commodity it seemed.

And yes, in the mix, as hard as it is to admit, I fell in love with her—an unexpected, complicated little wrench in my plan.

I keep replaying this morning—her flicking gaze, her trembling hands, the missing luggage...

The urge to flip a U-turn and head home is rampant, but I call her on my Bluetooth.

It goes straight to voicemail.

CHAPTER FIVE

LEVIN

"MADDY," I SAY WHEN I ANSWER HER CALL, "I'M READY."

There's no need for small talk. We both know what happened and what needs to happen. Details are neither here nor there.

"I'll meet you at Connor's," she says.

"See you in twenty." I hang up. Connor's is a diner a few miles away known for their pancakes and despised for their service.

I turn the burner off.

The other cell I hide in the closet, pressing it in one of my tennis shoes, a pair I've never

worn. If he tracks the location, it will still show I'm at home.

I don't glance back as I head outside exiting through the garage and walking down to where my rental car is waiting.

Alec will be on my trail soon enough, especially after a woman showed up at the house on his heels a few weeks ago.

I was home alone, drinking a glass of vino and watching mindless television—the kind you secretly love to hate—a group of bored housewives comparing their plastic surgery pitfalls and young, hunky boyfriends off to their frenemies.

The doorbell chimed.

I almost ignored it. No one would be looking for me. I kept to myself expecting no one.

A heavy knock echoed through the foyer into the den.

I grabbed the remote and hit pause on the DVR. I craned my neck to see who was peeking through the frosted glass of our double front doors.

The woman at the door was elegant. She was dressed to the nines in a printed wrap dress, Jimmy Choo's, and had Gucci shades piled on top of her blonde head.

I opened the door thinking she must be a Realtor.

She stuck her hand out. "You must be Levin Crowdley?" It came out as a question but sounded matter-of-fact, like she had known what to expect.

I nodded waiting for her to continue. She stared at me a moment too long.

"I'm Liz Hopkins, it's *wow*, crazy to meet you." She stumbles over her words. "You look so much like her. My sister." She searches my face to see if her name rings a bell. It does not.

"Do I know your sister?" I am confused. Is this a business acquaintance of Alec's?

"No." Liz pauses, "You don't. She's uh... she's gone."

I am curious. I don't know this woman but feel compelled to stand here and listen instead of slamming the door in her face. She isn't demented.

"You look like her," Liz repeats, shaking her head.

"I assume you know Alec, my fiancé?" I say.

"Only in passing." Liz fumbles over her next sentence. "I need to talk to you. I waited until he left."

My eyes narrow. Who is this woman? Did he have a long-lost sister I didn't know about?

Even worse, my mind turns a dark corner. You always hear about mistresses that confront the girlfriend or wife. Was her sister having an affair with Alec? I grab the door frame. The bile is rising in my throat. I instinctively reach for my throat, a nervous habit I have.

Liz reaches out for my arm. "I read online you got engaged. I had to warn you."

"We can't talk here." I nod up at the camera aimed right at the front door. I smile at her, the lens focused on us, trying not to look so tense.

"I look different," Liz says. "He won't know me. Here, I'm going to hand you my business card. It's actually a friend's." She hands me a card.

My hand shakes as I take it and make a point of reading it.

I look back up at her and smile. Janine Fredericks, Avon Consultant. I pretend I am making small talk. My mind races as I try to process what this could be about.

"Where can we talk?" Liz is apprehensive as she smooths a piece of hair down in a nervous gesture, now uncomfortable that she's being watched.

I pause, unsure of what to do, my thoughts racing in my head. Either this woman is certifiably crazy, or my fiancé is.

"Do you want to sit in my car?" Liz asks. There's nothing I want to do less.

I nod 'yes.'

Liz whispers. "I parked down the street. Meet me in fifteen. Act like you're going for a walk."

With that, she grabs my hand in an awkward handshake. She gives me a fake, toothy smile. She is beautiful. I drift back to her sister. What is she to Alec?

She turns, and I make it a point not to watch her walk

away. Alec would wonder why I did if he watches the tape, and I knew he did. He watches me like a hawk—eyes constant, darting back and forth on their prey, deciding when to swoop down for the kill.

I head inside and throw on some sweats and a tank top pretending I am going for a leisurely walk down the block. I even twist my hair into a knot on my head, which is now pounding with the uncertainties of what this strange woman has to tell me.

My stomach aches, and I start to gag. I make it to the toilet just in time to release the contents of tonight's dinner and wine.

There are moments in life that define you, that change you, for better or worse. In my gut, I knew this was one of those times.

I take my time reaching Liz Hopkin's safe navy Volvo down the street. It is a convertible, and I make a judgment call that says she prides herself on safety but wanted a little fun.

She sees me coming and unlocks the passenger side door.

I open it slowly. "I don't want to get in." I am not rude, but it is a firm commitment not to enter a stranger's vehicle.

She shakes her head in agreement. "Completely understand. Let me get out. We can talk here." Liz leaves her purse inside but takes her keys out. "Let's go for a walk."

I motion to her heels. "In those?"

She laughs—it is forced. I lean against her car. She does the same. We are facing each other not unlike a stand-off—the good vs. evil. I am unsure in this instance if there is a side.

"Was your sister having an affair with my fiancé?" The words are rushed and sound strange even to me. I swallow hard.

"Levin." She exhales, and I can tell what she has to tell me is tough for her. She searches my face. "Alec Durant is a killer. He murdered my younger sister."

The world starts to spin. My veins turn to ice like my whole body is frozen. My eyes get wide.

She continues, "Alec dated my sister in college at the University of Oklahoma. She was found dead her senior year of college. He was the last known person to see her."

I stare at her in disbelief. Pigs flying sounded more believable at this moment.

"Did he ever tell you about her?" she asks.

"Nooo." I am flabbergasted.

"Her name is, was, Heidi. Heidi Hopkins."

"She disappeared?"

"She didn't disappear. She was never lost." Liz looks at me hard. "Levin, do you want to sit?"

I can't speak. She clicks her keys and helps me into the passenger seat. I ease back into the cool leather, my skin matching the freezing temperature.

"I'm going to come around and sit." Liz shuts my door. She slides in and reaches for her purse. She pulls out her wallet and a tattered picture creased from being folded and unfolded. "This is Heidi." Her hands shake as she fingers the picture.

I make a motion to look at the picture. Liz is right, my doppelgänger is staring back at me. A gorgeous brunette with long legs and an even smile, and a smattering of freckles across the bridge of her nose. This is a cheerleading picture, and Heidi Hopkins is wearing a uniform, pom-poms in hand, looking like she doesn't have a care in the world.

Except now she is dead—at the hands of my fiancé.

"You need to leave and soon." Liz sounds like a concerned parent talking about an issue at the school bake sale, the chocolate chip cookies not organic or gluten-free. Not my life being turned upside down, the love of my life a cold-blooded girlfriend killer.

"What happened?" I don't want to know. I wish she wouldn't tell me. My palms are clammy, and I try to wipe them on my sweatpants.

"Eric, that's his name, right?" Liz reaches for my icy fingers, "I keep up with Alec. He was never charged, but his name came up in a *Google* search. I saw his business partner died. Then a year later, almost on the dot, he gets engaged to you." Liz holds my hands tight. "I had to warn you."

I think back to my relationship with Eric—the only solid friendship I ever had. He was my rock. I had watched him grow from a shy, introspective boy into a confident, outgoing, and sexy man. He had kept the qualities that made him irresistible to both sexes—a calming persona that could soothe even the most tempestuous of clients and associates and had been able to rein me in when I was on a destructive path during my adolescent years.

He tutored me, so I didn't fail out of high school after my mom had overdosed on pain medication. Though she claimed it was an accident, I had my suspicions. If I had her life, I would be looking for a respite from it all.

Eric's mistake, if one could categorize it as a mistake, was that he had fallen in love with a married man. The man's wife had unloaded on Alec. It didn't help that he had three young children and a dead-end marriage—the money was the root of the problem.

"When was this?" I manage to squeak out. My voice sounds foreign. A strangled cat would make more sense.

"This was their senior year of college, almost sixteen years ago." Liz wipes a tear from her eye. "She never came home to visit, and we knew... we knew something was wrong."

"How?" I close my eyes and lean my head back into the

headrest. A headache is migrating through my temples. I reach up and rub it.

"Heidi was choked to death." Liz is quiet as she gathers her thoughts. "Days later, she was found in her bed by her roommate. Her roommate had been visiting her boyfriend out of town for fall break."

"I don't understand..." My voice trails off. "I don't understand why you think this."

Liz looks at me with the most sorrowful eyes, pain apparent in the bright blue of her irises. "Levin, listen to me," her tone urgent. "You have to leave him. He killed my sister. I hired a PI who thinks he killed Eric. He's urging the authorities to re-open both cases."

I cut her off. "I want to go to the police, but Alec will know. He watches my every move. I need *something,* some proof."

"Yes, he's cunning." Liz shoves her keys in the ignition and starts the engine. "Heidi was going to leave Alec, and he murdered her. Eric was going to leave Alec, and he murdered him."

My head goes from pounding to throbbing to screaming.

"I have to go, he could be coming back shortly. We can't be seen talking, or this will be for nothing."

She has a valid point, but I am glued to the seat. The sweat is sticking to my back holding me in place.

"That card I gave you is for my friend and has a legit number. If you need to get in contact with me, call her. It won't look suspicious since she does sell beauty products." Liz is toying with another thought. "The police are going to re-open the case, Levin. When they do, I don't want you to be his next victim."

The chills shiver down my spine in succession. I manage to push open the door and force myself onto the sidewalk, the sun setting over another gorgeous San Diego day, no warning that behind that cloudless sky, there is a rapidly brewing storm.

CHAPTER SIX

ALEC

I START MY 8:00 A.M. CLIENT MEETING WITH AN AURA OF authority, impressing the client with my knowledge on the plat he's interested in and the ability to develop a parcel of land that he'd previously had zoning issues with. I spew out numbers, boredom creeping in, my brain on autopilot. Tell me something I don't know, I preface the client. Might've taken it a little too far, but I'm confident he likes my swagger.

Passing my secretary, Bridget's, desk, she flags me down with a question about dinner this evening. Her phone cradles her left shoulder, and she's deep in conversation wagging her finger in the air to get my attention. She refuses the idea of a headset, her argument being it makes her feel like she's working in a call center. I demur. She's the one running the place or gossiping. It's a toss-up, fifty-fifty if it's personal or professional.

She wants a count for the restaurant.

"Is Levin coming?" Bridget asks, nonchalant.

I feel my face start to burn, my temperature rising. I lower my eyes and shrug my shoulders.

"Alec?" she asks again, "Is Levin coming to dinner tonight?"

"I don't know," I say more cross than I intend.

Bridget looks at me nonplussed. "When will you?"

"She's not feeling well." I lie.

She sighs. "Let me know later?"

Bridget knows my moods. She takes my sigh to mean that she should leave me the hell alone. She looks down at her computer screen to halt the conversation. I can get through to Bridget without much effort.

Who I couldn't seem to get through to was Levin.

I still couldn't reach her.

Levin knows better than to disappear or to ghost me.

This behavior, disconcerting as it is, prompts me to contact George, my private investigator, the one I keep around just in case. In life, there are always those just-in-case moments that give you pause. There is no price on a man who can take your secrets to the grave.

He doesn't answer. I hang up.

We don't leave voicemails or a trail. I'll try him back later.

I speed dial Levin one more time. Her sing-song voice cuts through the unrest in my head, rapid-fire thoughts coming my way.

"This is Levin Crowdley, leave a message." I'd heard that greeting a thousand times before, but today it rattled me. The anger was starting to rise, the flush creeping up my neck.

Half a dozen messages and no calls back, I feel like a pubescent boy waiting on a date for the prom, already knowing the girl of his dreams has said no but hasn't relayed the message to him.

I call her gym. They say she's canceled her appointment today.

Trying the animal shelter next, no one answers. I let it ring at least twenty times before giving up.

Did Levin know about Eric?

Or was this about my quest to have a baby?

I didn't expect Levin to be upset when I told her I threw her birth control pills out last week. She could barely remember what day of the week it was, so I thought she would be relieved that she didn't have to remember to take a pill every day.

With my fortieth birthday fast approaching, I was starting to consider our fertility, and namely, my ability to procreate. I would also be grateful for the inheritance our child would stand to receive based upon Eric's will if Levin got married and had children.

In high school, my girlfriend and I didn't use condoms, and she never got pregnant.

Tara, a girl I hooked up with on and off throughout college, was never on birth control. Our drunken hook-ups were legendary in my frat house, especially since she was a bicycle—ridden by everyone—a shared secret with my Sigma Phi brothers.

Then there was Heidi. Heidi Hopkins, who broke my heart. Heidi had an abortion. I found out it was someone else's. The college rumor mill had given away this priceless piece of information.

After the procedure, she was going to leave me. She was going to leave me. The baby wasn't mine. I lost all sensibilities. I was cut out of her life, just like that. All the big moments in life, I'm on the sidelines.

Take Eric for example. He was trying to sever ties with me when he died. The business we founded he wanted me to walk away from, like an absentee parent.

I didn't want Levin to find out, but she's the beneficiary. I had no choice.

I had been cut out of the will, so I was also provided a copy as standard procedure. 'Disinherited,' they called it. I called it 'highway robbery.' I saw red, the instinct to get my hands around Eric's neck a thrilling idea.

My idea had been to get married as soon as possible foregoing a long engagement. For once, time was a luxury even I couldn't afford. Eric was our link, the lifeline that connected Levin and me.

I'd met Eric in grad school, and we'd opened our business together shortly after. His dad had been our investor, our biggest supporter.

After Eric died, his parents and I agreed to stay in touch. I was like a third son to them, though more like a second since the other son was a royal fuck-up. Eric's older brother, Brad, was in drug rehab for the fourth time, and it didn't look like this time would stick either. He had missed the funeral because his heroin addiction had spiraled out of control yet again. His parents had spent countless dollars on trying to clean him up, and, if I might add, wasted money that could have been better spent on our business endeavors. A pair of shoes was more worthwhile to invest in than Brad's cleanliness. Better return on investment, if you asked me.

Being close to his parents also allowed me to keep them close in case I needed to be privy to any information they had regarding his death. It also provided me the opportunity to ask Eric's dad for money if I needed it in a pinch.

If Levin left, there would be serious consequences. My entire plan would crumble. All of this would have been for nothing.

I check the GPS tracker app installed on my phone.

According to this, the Range Rover is in the garage.

My palms sweat. I wipe them on my desk.

Maybe she has a man in the house? My temperature

inches upward and internally, my blood boils. My hands ball into tight fists as I clench and unclench them. My jaw is set.

I log into my computer tapping my fingers on the keyboard. There are video cameras all over the house. The security system shows me the available cameras in and around the house.

No Levin.

I'm able to go back, and I watch her leave. She goes out the garage, no backward glance, nothing. Her vehicle is still in the driveway.

My fingers are a steeple as I consider her whereabouts.

One does not reach this level of success in life by being lackadaisical.

For this reason, I keep tabs on Levin. She is, after all, my greatest asset.

The journal I keep on her is imperative to our growth as a couple and her as my fiancée.

I fish the key for my desk drawer out of the bottom of an envelope on my bookshelf.

I reach down in my mahogany desk drawer and pull out the black moleskin journal I keep on Levin. It's buried beneath some old financial documents and outdated real estate magazines.

The pages are creased and starting to show my frenzied pace on taking notes.

Levin's diet. Levin's eating habits. What our chef prepares. What I dislike her eating because it hurts her stomach. The types of seafood she can tolerate—salmon is disgusting and fishy to her, but tuna tartare is edible. Her periods. Mood swings. Medication. She has to take Xanax for her anxiety at times. I note her depression. Unsurprising, really, with the upbringing she had. This could all be useful someday.

The most important part of my black book—Levin's

schedule. The days she volunteers at the animal shelter (Monday, Wednesday, and Friday). Her gym classes (Barre, Abs on Fire, Cardio Cinch), and her trainer's name (Andrew Metz, the Greek God trainer).

She rarely mentions any friends. Her family is all dead—probably for the best—deadbeats.

She doesn't need any other commitments or any other priorities taking her away from me. She's all mine, just the way I like it.

Her passwords would be the most important except those are committed to memory. Her email, voicemail, and PIN for her ATM card are all stored up top.

I write a few notes on her behavior today, biting my lip as I think about the morning. Oh dear, I hope this isn't going to become a pattern. I get up and place the tiny silver key back in the envelope and hide it back on the bookshelf.

My thoughts are racing, re-playing her actions today. I impatiently tap my fingers on the desk.

Maybe she's meeting someone. That Andrew Metz guy—her trainer—but not to work out.

A heart attack is imminent for the direction my mind is headed.

Money, I think to myself. Money is the common denominator with everything in life. You either have it, or you don't.

Bingo. Time for a check of Levin's bank account.

Lucky for me, the president of the bank is my friend, an old golf chum of mine, and as soon as she set up that account, he assured me I'd be privy to it. I know what she spends her money on—every dime of it. Usually, it's for her own choice in clothing or basic necessities.

There are large withdrawals over the last few days. The current balance is $.01.

I inhale, my stomach is queasy. I put my head between my

legs wanting to rip my computer off the desk and smash it into pieces.

Like a car accident you can't pry your eyes from, I log in to the cell phone account, knowing I'm not going to like the results.

There are no outgoing calls today, but her cell phone is in my name, and I note the amount of unknown numbers and blocked caller IDs on the bill.

I call her cell again. It goes straight to voicemail. This time, I punch in her password on the keypad and tap my pen, the irritation apparent by the loud thwacks as it hits the desk. I hold my breath as I wait to hear how many voicemails she has since yesterday afternoon when I last checked.

Andrew Metz, her twenty-eight-year-old buff trainer that resembles Zac Efron, the *Baywatch* version, has left her a message. He called her a half hour ago about her missed appointment.

"Hey, sweetie, this is Andy. We missed each other this morning. I don't like when you miss," he clears his throat and pauses for an awkward silence. "I need to see you soon."

I slam the phone back in the cradle and lean back in my chair, hard enough that I almost somersault backward onto the plush beige carpeting of my office.

That whore is cheating.

Levin Crowdley had said yes and made a commitment when I slipped a ring on her finger.

I knew it was a surprise to her. I saw the way her face reacted and her body shook. She had no idea it was coming, maybe she didn't even know it was what she wanted.

But she had to want it because I did.

I own her now. She's mine.

The stakes are too high to let her go.

I pick up the phone and dial.

I have one more call to make.

The phone rings twice before a woman comes on and asks me to hold. The silence is palpable, and my eyes drift. I can't help but glance at the silver and gold-plated picture frame on the corner of my desk. It is one of the happiest days of my life—Levin and I standing outside of the house I had purchased for us. I am standing with my arm around her as the white stucco looms behind us, symbolic of how far I have come up in this world.

The guy gets the house and the girl.

I think back to a few months ago when I had picked out a house for us.

I knew it wasn't exactly her style, but it was mine. The massive floor plan was guaranteed to give me a hard-on. I liked big. The bigger, the better.

Some might say I have a short-man complex. I prefer to call it drive and determination. When you have money, who cares what complex you have?

The house was over four thousand square feet complete with a pool, hot tub, cabana, and built-in BBQ. It was an entertainer's paradise.

The furniture was mainly glass and black leather and included in the sale of the house. Various surfaces had shiny, slick surfaces that showed every fingerprint smudge but looked expensive. I knew this decorum would be replaced with more sensible tastes when a baby came, but that was a price I was willing to pay for the greater good. I'd sacrifice it all to ensure my plan worked.

The only part of the house that piqued her interest was the pergola in the backyard. It provided shade, and it was her peaceful retreat. She spent her time with a book in hand, lounging on a patio chair, sometimes comfortable with Hemingway, on the flipside King, and she loved the shade it provided.

Within thirty days, it was ours. The morning we closed,

finalized the paperwork, and received the keys was etched into my memory. I headed into the office to work for a few hours, and she managed the movers.

Just an ordinary, happy couple moving into their dream home one cardboard box at a time.

When I came home, she was naked on the counter, Christian Louboutin heels on her feet, red bottoms pointing up, waiting for me to taste every inch of her skin. Her dark hair flowed on the quartz countertops, a coquettish gleam in her bright, green eyes as I undid my belt, unzipped my pants, and took her right there. She nuzzled my neck and nibbled my earlobe as I explored every inch of her body. I held her arms over her head pushing my way into her engorged lips and watched her face as she came multiple times.

I got hard just thinking about it, my penis tightening as I thought about the control I had over her. I owned her, every square inch of her five-foot-seven stature. She might as well be a piece of real estate I was trying to develop. I had put my time and money into her, and she would pay dividends, especially now that I knew it was the only way out of my financial woes. She would be found, and she would be mine. I could not lose out on the ability to save myself from a money meltdown now that it was easy.

Marry Levin.

Have babies.

Get disgustingly rich in the process.

CHAPTER SEVEN

LEVIN

I PULL INTO THE GRAVEL DRIVEWAY AT CONNOR'S JUST before 10:00 a.m. The breakfast crowd has dissipated, just the way Maddy and I want it. I drive around to the back of the building where her maroon Honda Civic is parked near the edge of the lot.

She climbs out of her car and heads over to my driver's side window, her dark hair swept up in a messy bun, and her usual mom-iform of sweats and a tank top covers her doughy body. The flush on her cheeks suggests she's already been to the gym this morning.

"How are ya?" She leans in the window and kisses my cheek.

I offer a tight smile. "I'm just ready to leave. I hope one of these nights I can sleep again."

"You will," she promises. "Your whole life's ahead of you. No use in wasting your time with a suppressive person."

Maddy hands me an envelope. "What's this?" I knit my eyebrows. "It better not be a lottery ticket. I never win."

She laughs and playfully slaps my arm. "This is the key to your rental."

"This doesn't feel like a key." I shake the envelope and hear metal clicking, but it is heavier than just a set of keys.

"Doug and I thought you could use some extra funds." Doug was her husband and a big, exuberant man who had a similar heart of gold.

"Maddy," I say. "No. You keep it."

"Absolutely not," her voice is firm and unrelenting. "You take it and get the hell out of here. Away from that asshole."

"Thank you." I look at her, a tear threatens to squeeze out.

"Let me know if you need me to extend the car rental."

"Okay. I'll try and get a vehicle in the next few days," I say. I'd pulled all the money out of my account so that I could buy a cheap one in cash.

"Don't use your phone if you don't have to," she warns, "but let me know when you arrive. You should reach Phoenix later tonight. I'm guessing by five or six if you don't hit too much traffic."

I nod. There's nothing more I can say without crying. I don't deserve their generosity, but I'll be forever grateful for it.

Maddy grabs the door handle of the Impala and opens it. She reaches in and gives me a hard, tight hug.

"Be safe," she whispers, her voice choked. I wrap my arms around her neck. All twenty-six years of my life in preparation for this—running from another man who wished me harm.

My dad had left when I was in grade school, an alcoholic who was searching for Jesus in the arms of his AA sponsor. He was replaced by faceless men who had no part in my life other than to lock me in my room so they could make my mother scream in pain or pleasure.

We hadn't had a fancy life, but it had been middle class. We had lived on a tree-lined street in a ranch home. I had my own bedroom furnished with my daybed and my favorite toys.

Dad had been a manager at an auto parts store, and Mom had been in charge of a medical billing office. Together they had made ends meet. We had taken a few family vacations in the minivan over the summers. We hadn't been rich, but we hadn't been poor.

They had once been happy, I remember it. I hold onto it like a hand that is barely touching mine, fingers once intertwined but starting to unravel.

Everything spiraled out of control when my dad lost his parents in succession—his father had succumbed to cirrhosis of the liver, and within another six months, his mother had died after an automobile accident. What had been a few cocktails with his dinner had turned to happy hour after work and had continued throughout the night.

My mother tried to keep the façade of a happy marriage up. She would hide alcohol bottles from him—and from me. Their arguments that had once been few and far between had turned continual and ugly. The bottles would pile up. I would find them stuck in the hall closet behind folded sheets, under the sink in the bathroom behind my strawberry-scented bubble bath, and even in the tool shed behind the pliers.

My dad had screamed at her, called her every name in the book in his drunken rages, but he had never raised a hand to her that I knew of.

After my dad left, she shacked up with Jeff, subsequently losing her job at the medical billing office after she started coming in with black eyes and split lips. They said it's bad for business.

Jeff had a temper. Whereas my dad would yell and then black out in the middle of a rant, Jeff was conniving and mean. He didn't like it if other men paid attention or glanced at her. Their nights out would turn into screaming and hitting matches with my mother being the punching bag every time. I would try to stay with friends, but Jeff kept coming around more and more.

At first, he also showered me with attention. He liked to play daddy. He would ask me to sit on his lap, tell me I could be his girl and would try to impress me with magic tricks and jokes. He told my mom he wanted to be involved in my life—maybe coaching a softball team or taking me to the park.

But it was all smoke and mirrors. Jeff lived for free at his apartment since he was the maintenance man. I would cover my face with a pillow when they would stumble in drunk or I would hear them making animal noises in the bedroom. Anything was preferable to the screaming and thuds that became a weekly, then almost an every other day occurrence.

And then it got worse. I didn't think it could get any worse. But I was wrong.

CHAPTER EIGHT

ALEC

I TRY THE PI FOR THE SECOND TIME, MY ANNOYANCE palpable and a hard ball lodged in my throat. It takes four rings for him to answer. I'm lucky he's the most loyal and conniving bastard I know.

"George, it's me," I pause. "She's gone.

My private investigator grunts on the other end. "I'm on it."

There's no elaboration needed or names given.

"I'm thinking she flew. The vehicle is supposedly in the garage unless she found out about the tracker."

George is always available, never takes vacations, and seems to admire my work ethic and need to get rid of those in my way. He shares the same philosophy as I do, and he's taking my secrets to the grave. For that reason alone, he's indispensable and bankrolled.

A former military sergeant, a cop, and an ex-con, though that came later, he'd been the one who suggested a tracking device on her vehicle going so far as to order and install it himself.

Before I proposed to Levin, he had done a lengthy background check on her. I didn't want any surprises. She was a typical white trash girl who grew up with nothing—no parents, no money, no roots. She'd been a member of the cheerleading squad, track, dance, volunteered at a local women's shelter, and worked waitressing jobs. In college, she graduated cum laude with a 3.85 GPA. Her desire to travel had led her on a journey to Europe to explore what the U.S.A. couldn't offer.

The addresses piled up over the years. She'd lived all over—apartments, trailers, houses. The only physical house attached to her background was foreclosed on when she was seven, yet here she was running away from a life most could only dream of.

How could I have misjudged the situation so poorly? How could I have lost the upper hand? All control?

She's going to pay for hurting my feelings. It's the only solution, the only way to get my head above water again.

I fantasize about finding Levin, and it scares me how vivid the memory of Heidi's death is. I picture my hands gripping her neck, squeezing, and letting myself lose control. I imagine Heidi's face, the look of terror, her neck purple and mottled, but the eyes are Levin's—green, shiny emeralds—that lose their luster as the air is sucked out by the arms controlling her last breath.

I realize I'm holding my breath. I let out a gentle gasp forcing myself to snap back to reality.

I head home after talking to George. I'll let him take care of Levin. At least for now.

As expected, the Range Rover is in the garage. Parked in the same spot. It hasn't moved.

My heart races as I walk through the empty house.

Nothing seems so out of place that a stranger would notice, but I did. The missing clothes, jewelry, and her favorite fuzzy blue blanket.

What about the engagement ring? I punch a wall, the drywall giving way to a gaping hole. The imperfection makes me seethe. I pull my fist out and cradle it.

I need to calm down. I take a deep breath. Then another.

My comfort should have been the nursery, but even that room seems bare and uncaring. The neutral colors and gender-neutral palette do nothing to ease my tension.

Until something glimmers catching my eye.

To my chagrin, the light reflecting off the crib is her engagement rock nestled in the sheets.

Tearing through the house, I heave the quintessential books off of the glass coffee table in the living room and smash the decorative vase in the den.

I kick walls—a tantrum the understatement of the year. Scuff marks and scratches are now visible on the eggshell paint where I kick my Gucci loafers.

The baby's room would have to have a new changing table as I use my fist to pummel the wood until it splinters. The dishes in the sink leftover from Levin's absenteeism would have to be replaced, their bright colors now in broken bits on the travertine tile from where I drop them in a pile, the soothing noise of shattering glass a lullaby to my ears.

It is a relief Levin isn't here to see me like this, though this was all her fault.

"You fucking bitch." I pound on the kitchen countertop. I don't yell, but say it in a whisper glaring toward the pictures of us on the mantle. "Burn in hell."

I smash a glass against the wall and watch it shatter like the façade of my life.

At that moment, if given the chance, I would have

smashed her face in. I rip up a picture of her that is on the fridge. After tearing it into bits, I throw it in the garbage can.

I am done.

Finished.

The air deflates from my lungs as I crumble to the floor.

I don't bother to clean up any of the mess I made. I'd call someone to remove the broken crib legs and the busted dishes, but they'll ask what happened at the house, and I don't want any questions or witnesses to my outburst.

I'll say we had an intruder. The worst kind. Same difference.

What the hell was she thinking? How could she drop her engagement ring in the crib and take off without a backward glance?

I'm pensive, pulling at my tie like it's causing me to lose my breath. I loosen it and think, does she know? I've made sure to watch her closely. Could she have found out about Eric? The thought fills me with dread, and I tug the tie until it unravels in my hand. What if she plans on going to the authorities before I can catch her?

When I make it to the client dinner at Bradshaw's, my temper is in check. The house is now in shambles due to my frustration, but I have calmed down.

"Hi," I say to the hostess dressed in a skimpy black dress that might as well be a negligee. "Party of three, reservation under Durant, Alec Durant."

She smiles at me. "Yes, Mr. Durant. Glad to see you made it. However, Mr. Williams called, and he can't make dinner."

My smile freezes on my lips. The client called the steakhouse and not *me* to cancel?

"Did he happen to mention why?" I keep my tone level.

"No." The hostess is already bored with this conversation anxious to tend to the next patron. "I can seat you at the table you reserved if you'd like."

"No," I say. "I'll head to the bar." I saunter over to the middle of the restaurant where the bar is situated and take a seat. Once there, I motion to the bartender. "Gin and tonic. Double."

He nods as if he understands what it's like to be the poor schmuck at the bar ordering multiple drinks and waiting on no one.

"Seventeen dollars." He slides the drink over to me.

"I'll start a tab." I pull my black card out of my wallet.

"Let me know when you're ready for the next round." He takes the card. I might as well have handed him a tip jar filled with twenty dollar bills. My AMEX is the key to better treatment at most places. I wouldn't be able to pay the fees if I didn't get my money from Eric's estate via Levin's generosity. The money *I* deserved.

I sigh, the annoyance palpable on my face as my mouth settles into a hard line. I want to sit and cry, but I can't. I feel dead inside, the way my ex-girlfriend felt when I strangled her to death. I don't want to go back to that period in my life. I wring my hands on the bar taking a huge swig of my drink. I slam it down on the counter. Damn, this is not how I thought this night would go.

The bartender didn't even wait for me to ask, he brought me another double. There was no conversation necessary, just the glass sliding across the smooth wood into my hand.

I feel a tap on my shoulder. Immediately, my mind goes to Levin. It's not her. It's my canceled dinner date, Mr. Roger Williams.

"Hey, sorry I'm late," Roger says shrugging his shoulders. "I told them to tell you I was running late."

My eyes are slits as I look back toward the hostess stand

—that dumb bitch. I can't get angry or let Roger see me lose my composure.

"Fifty bucks if you move," I say to the woman beside me who is clearly waiting on a date that isn't coming. She has been checking her phone and watch along with the clock in the bar for the last half hour. She glares at me but grabs her clutch and stands up, wavering on cheap, five-inch stilettos. I toss a crisp 'Grant' at her, the former president's face stoic, a spitting image of my demeanor, and wave my hand at Roger.

Roger takes her place as she painfully exits the bar, one clomp after another like a Clydesdale horse, unsteady on her feet. He orders a whiskey sour and turns to me. "I thought you were bringing someone?" The question isn't meant to conjure up hard feelings, but it does. I grip my glass and swallow. "Levin. My fiancée. Yeah, she's not feeling well. I think she gave herself food poisoning."

Roger's eyes get wide. "Hopefully not trying to poison you."

He's joking, and I laugh.

"She's not the best cook," I say. "I tolerate it though because she's hot."

Now it is his turn to laugh—and he does— and though we make small talk for a few minutes, the conversation is stilted.

The hostess, realizing her fuck-up, comes over and offers us a prime table. We follow her to a booth—red leather and dark mahogany with dim lighting—in the back of the restaurant.

Our waitress comes over and offers us a cocktail. I don't mean to shoot daggers her way, but she's a dead ringer for Levin. Her brunette hair is long and shiny, and her green eyes stand out against her olive skin.

Roger's droning on about politics and shit I could care less about—dead presidents and current presidents have no place in our discussion. I try to pay attention, but my mind keeps wandering to Levin—is she in bed with someone? My eyes narrow to slits, and Roger stops in the middle of a tirade on NAFTA.

"You okay, Alec?" His face shows concern, the wrinkles giving way to his overtly white veneers.

I shake my head.

"Yes, I'm just thinking of the points you're making..." I drown my cocktail and continue, "because you bring up some valid concerns."

I try and transition the conversation into business—our real estate development venture.

My worst fears are confirmed—Roger isn't interested in negotiating a deal. If Levin had been here, she would have been the smooth conversationalist. She would have found talking points and commonalities. I notice a gold wedding band on his ring finger. She would have asked about his wife. I open my mouth to ask when the waitress comes over—the Levin lookalike. Un-fucking-believable.

Roger launches into his real estate concerns, but I'm done listening—my mind is on Levin again.

I glance at my phone. No missed calls. Not one.

I can't handle any more of the run-around. I interrupt Roger, "I gotta go." I lie, lifting my phone. "Levin needs me."

Roger's brows rise at my abruptness.

"She isn't holding down any fluids. She says she feels weak," I add. "I'm going to run her to the ER."

Roger nods. "Oh, God, go. Be there for the better half. They're always there for us."

I settle up with the waitress as I walk by, and she quickly runs my card as I stare at her ass—dead ringer for Levin's. The waitress introduces herself as 'Kodi,' guessing twenty-five years old, fake tits that are large enough to spill over her mandatory black bustier but small enough to question whether they're real or not. Her small waist is attached to long legs and an ass that walks away like Levin's, a slight sashay to her walk.

Of-fucking-course.

I make it to the corner bar and sit crooked on a rickety stool unsure if it can support the weight of my thoughts and me. My mind is on Levin and where she went. I flicker back and forth between today and the last few months pressing myself on any indicators she would leave.

The night passes as I watch the crowd around me fill the bar stools and then empty out, each face being replaced by another one. Some are happy, some lackadaisical, some boisterous, some arguing over the dumb shit couples argue over—babysitters and work issues.

I reach for my wallet, the leather sitting next to my ambitious third round at this particular juncture. As I put it back in my pocket, I realize the engagement ring is nestled in my other back pocket. I finger it through the thin fabric of my dress pants. The first thing I'm going to do when I see her again is put it back where it belongs. I clench and unclench my hand, the pricelessness of squeezing the last breath out of her ungrateful lips. The want is so bad I can taste it on my lips, and I bite down hard until I feel blood. I taste it, and it calms me, the bitterness a gentle reminder of how she's going to pay for this.

There's no way I can drive the Audi home. The bartender offers an Uber, but I prefer a cab tonight. I am not in the mood for incessant chattering or questions. A buff bodybuilder type in faded blue jeans and a V-neck tee is out front when I stumble through the doors of the restaurant, thumping into the glass with a loud bang. He looks in the rearview mirror as I manage to thrust the heavy metal door open and half-crawl, half jump inside.

He takes into account my bloodshot eyes and my disheveled appearance—my tie askew and my hair mussed from running my hands through it. There is no judgment, as caustic as it sounds, he's used to my type—businessmen in bars, some celebrating, some deprecating right on the spot—taking them home to their families, to their mistresses, to their dealer's house for another snort of cocaine.

I'm not unusual and because of that, not a threat. His dark eyes focus back on the street ahead. His hands grip the steering wheel, and he commences his conversation with whoever is on the other end of the phone. I am relieved.

At the driveway of my house, I pay him in cash and an extra twenty for his troubles. He is appreciative but stoic, a slight turn of his head the only indication he is grateful. It takes me a couple tries to get the key in the lock. It is times like these I wish I had my garage door opener with me. I enter the house, cold and uninviting, and I am reminded all over again of Levin and how she left, the broken furniture a remnant of my earlier feelings.

The closet hadn't fared so well. It looks like a scorned lover—empty and desolate—the way I felt now that she left. It smells like her—the Chanel perfume she wears a lingering whiff in the large walk-in closet. Her clothing, shoes, and purses are all arranged according to their color. Jeans are folded on a shelf, same with her plain t-shirts and gym attire. I grab a Missoni scarf from the rack and smell it, burying my face in the zig-zag pattern of the fabric, the loss of her strangling me just like this scarf around her neck if I used it correctly.

I slide down to the carpeted floor wondering what Levin is doing at this very moment.

Halfheartedly, I toss a few pairs of shoes creating chaos in her orderly space, ruining the line-up of matched pairs. I'm about to chuck another shoe, this time, a tennis one, when I feel extra weight, something tucked in the front of the shoe.

I shake it. Levin's phone slides back, the case, a picture of us—smiling, happy, newly engaged.

Biting my lip, I type in her passcode. It doesn't work. Sighing, I try it again. Still incorrect.

Her passcode changed since yesterday. The location services were on all this time, a decoy so I would think she was home. I slam her phone down in my hand after trying a few guesses.

Her birthday.

Mine.

Eric's.

This is a problem for George, he'll have to break into her phone.

My mind wanders to tonight. She should've been at dinner. Instead, I come home to an empty house that seems all the more vacant, the missing items taunting me in their absence.

I toss and turn in our king bed that now feels enormous—empty—like my insides. The ones she ripped clear out.

To think we had almost nailed down a wedding date.

She suggested a destination wedding since Eric was gone. I wanted a big, overblown wedding with a top-notch caterer, a videographer, a live band, and an impressive venue—something to show I was serious about this. About her. Us.

Her mind is made up, stubbornness rearing its ugly head as she's adamant we follow *her* wishes. She hadn't hired a wedding planner or taken on the responsibility. I should've known she was having second thoughts. I suppose I didn't want to see it then and didn't want to accept that something wasn't going according to my plan.

I was frustrated then, wanting to get the show on the road. There was a need to breathe new life into my business. People love weddings—the celebration of two becoming one, the cake, the dancing, the vows.

The vows got me every time.

Promise to have and to hold until death do us part.

I would keep that vow despite the fact we've yet to say those words aloud. I figure they're implied. She said 'yes,' didn't she?

My mind goes into overdrive, a mental picture of us at our wedding.

Initially, a large but intimate wedding was the plan, at least for me. I had a lot of business associates and making them feel like one of the family was the goal. If they felt like part of my life and not just dollar signs, it would bode well for business.

Levin had been adamant she didn't want that. I thought I would persevere and win. I always did, especially when I used money as the main objective or pointed out that her lavish lifestyle cost lots of money.

She never asked for the things I gave her, but that didn't matter.

I knew we could work through whatever problems she had. I just hoped it wasn't about Eric.

She would see that this was a mistake—her leaving me—I would make sure of that.

I fall into a restless sleep, tossing and turning.

My cell buzzes next to me on the nightstand. The digital numbers on the alarm clock say 3:00 a.m. I fumble as I reach for it. The caller ID says unknown.

It better be Levin.

"George." The voice on the other end is gruff.

I say nothing, wallowing in the sound of his heavy breathing.

"Found her in Arizona. In a rental car. Impala," George pauses. "She's in a hotel tonight. A Super 8 in the South Phoenix area. Shady as fuck."

"A Super 8?" I'm incredulous. The idea of her in a budget

motel sleeping on the comforter, so she doesn't have to get in the bed is almost asinine.

"Arizona," I repeat it. Random. As far as I know, she doesn't have ties there unless she's fucking some Phoenician idiot. One of those men who brag about hiking and the mountain trails they can ride, all while carrying one hundred pounds of water and useless camping shit on their back.

George hangs up, promising he'll email me the details.

I throw the phone down. Sleep is useless at this point.

Arizona. That might be the ideal spot for our wedding.

I get up tossing the covers off and stubbing my toe on the edge of the bed, but I feel nothing. I'm too distracted.

My phone chimes twice. George's email and my flight itinerary.

The travel bag's in the closet, and I throw some clothes and my toiletries in and zip it shut. I swallow some aspirin and Uber a ride to the airport.

Precious time has already been wasted, her phone a red herring.

I need her back with me.

After all, she's mine.

CHAPTER NINE

Levin

The drive to Phoenix was virtually a straight shot down the I-10.

Even though this area's notoriously unbearable in the summer, it still seems like a good choice. Alec hated the desert. To him, it's suburbia hell, an oven that never cools down, and he couldn't imagine life without the ocean nearby. The heat strangled him, and he called Phoenix a 'desperate wannabee California.'

Anywhere is a better idea than sleeping next to a murderous ex-fiancé.

The five-hour drive wasn't terrible, but my nerves were shot. My hands grew tired from clutching the steering wheel, and my eyes kept darting to my mirrors every time a car lingered too close.

My car rolls into a half-empty parking lot at a Super 8 in a seedy area since the vacation rental lease doesn't technically start until tomorrow, I decide this will do. My eyes are heavy and sleep-deprived, and I need to be able to function tomorrow.

Tomorrow's the only day I have to settle in before I start my new job. Maddy's cousin works at a resort in Paradise Valley tucked into the breathtaking mountains, and it turned out they're looking to fill a new position. Catering to high-end clientele, mostly athletes, movie stars, and new-money types seeking beautiful seclusion, Alec won't think to look for me here. Maddy's boss is notorious for hiring cheap labor and paying them under the table which is what I needed—a job with no W-2 or paper trail for Alec to find me. Getting a job there required her cousin's help, but the fact that I embellished my resume to reflect previous hotel management and au pair experience made me a prime candidate

I was going to be cleaning rooms and running errands for the guests. It was a small resort with only twenty villas. It caters to the elitist generation by focusing on one-to-one personalized attention that results in guests feeling like they have their own assistant.

For this reason, there was one household helper for every four rooms. We have to provide the utmost in customer service, and they need us to focus on our unforgiving clientele who could ruin their reputation if given bad service.

At this moment, I'm in the opposite position trying not to picture rooms rented by the hour or the cockroach that crawled on the broken tile in the bathroom. I manage to lie down on the queen-size flowered bed.

The bed is squishy and uncomfortable as I rest my body on the outside of the comforter. It looks like it's never been washed and reeks of cigarette smoke and bad decisions, a painful reminder of my childhood and the apartment we shared with my mom's boyfriend when I was nine years old.

When men touched me, I could pretend. I could try to forget all the hurt and anger and the marks from my childhood. I did a good job at forgetting for a moment and letting them get their satisfaction.

But I didn't. My mind was always back to a place in the distance. It was always looking behind me. I remembered him. How he had first been warm to me, asking me questions, buying me little trinkets like bracelets and glitter and My Little Ponies. I thought he was different. Nice.

Mother had introduced him to me as 'Jeff.' He was the handyman in our apartment complex. It was a sad little place. We'd recently lost our home to foreclosure after Dad left. We were sharing a small, one-bedroom apartment at the time. Mother was still working then as a cashier at the grocery store. Smoking and life choices hadn't hardened her, hadn't yet broken her spirit or taken over her body. The string of bad relationships hadn't become the status quo yet.

Jeff had stopped by to fix our leaky faucet in the kitchen. While he was there, he'd hung some pictures and replaced the broken screens on the windows. I was nine the first time I met him, still impressionable and trusting. My mom had been so thrilled that Jeff had taken a liking to her, to me.

It was not the liking a man should have taken to a little girl.

Nausea floods my body. I run to the bathroom to throw-up—my nerves shot, my head pounding. I don't want to go back in the past. And as much as I don't want to think about Alec, it is impossible to get him out of my head. When I met Alec, I thought he could save me from my history. I was crazy to think he could love me. *Truly* love me.

If there's anything I've learned so far in life, it's that a man's love is incapable of being genuine. They always want something. They're only ever in it for themselves. Silly me for thinking Alec was different.

Alec always had to outdo everyone and everything. If he decided he wanted marriage, it was a done deal. If he felt a baby would complete the picture, it was landscaped into our future. I never questioned it because I thought he loved me. I thought he knew what was best for us.

At first, I admired his ambition. He didn't drink excessively, and he seemed to care about building a business and longevity. He took an interest in my hobbies and what I was passionate about, at first supportive of my dreams.

Then the red flags became glaringly obvious—he didn't want me to work outside the home, he wanted me to play 'wifey' and coddle him. His drinking wasn't to the extent of my father's, but it became apparent that copious amounts of alcohol were involved in the day-to-day of Alec Durant. This was an obvious concern considering once my dad started the bottle, he never stopped. The trajectory was long and hard. I do give my mother credit for sticking by him long after the alcohol took over. Eventually, he lost his job because he started hiding bottles in his desk, then showing up late, then not at all.

His face became red—at first, it was questionable if it was the liquor or his anger. He became bloated, sickly looking, and sweated profusely. I looked at him and recognized a stranger. He went from getting up at 7:00 a.m. and making me breakfast to sitting lazily on the couch flipping the channels while holding a whiskey sour.

The pungent smell of it makes me gag to this day. This is probably why I only have the occasional drink. It is the devil to me in liquid form. The purest kind of evil there is.

He started hitting my mother. The fights became fight or flights, run-for-your-life types. There was no more love in the house. It had died. It wasn't long before the word 'separation' and 'divorce' became a topic of discussion. After my dad lost his job, he never left the couch. It became his temple where he slept, ate, and drank. Until one day, he up and left. The house was foreclosed. He died in a Seattle homeless shelter, a sad and angry waste of a man.

Eric knew this, and so did Alec. I had nightmares that would result in me finding my father passed out on the street, toothless and begging out of a Styrofoam cup, and he doesn't know it's me. He refuses my help and my money. I see his haunted eyes, but they don't recognize me. It shakes me to my core every time becoming a stranger to my father.

Speaking of strangers, I've been sleeping beside a savage—one that I thought I knew and loved. I shudder as I think of him lying next to me at night, while I dream of our future, he's thinking of his past and the lives he ruined.

Or not. They say murderers don't always feel remorse. They're narcissistic.

Alec would eventually find the ring in the crib. It might take him a minute, but he would come into the room and try to destroy the crib because it was a reminder of me. Our baby. Our life.

I don't think anyone had ever left him until Heidi tried and then Eric and now me. My body started to shake. The comforter was threadbare and did nothing to help the chills subside. I curled myself into a ball.

The sobs start to wrack my body as I realize that everyone close to Alec has died. If he finds me, there is a good chance I won't live to see another day. The realization as it dawns on me causes me to cry myself into submission, the comforter now soaked with my tears.

It is at this exact moment that I want to run into the arms of a big, strong police officer who can lock Alec away for life.

But I can't.

Not yet.

I need proof.

CHAPTER TEN

Alec

The airport is dead, just like Levin if she doesn't follow through on the marriage proposal. I lean back in first class and think about my life, my history, my family, and the loved ones I've lost.

No one has ever left me and got away with it.

When my parents moved halfway across the country, I had to teach them a lesson. It was an invaluable one, at least to me. They lost their lives when I cut their brakes back when the sensors on your car didn't provide you with diagnostics on what was wrong. I scowl at the thought of how smart our technology has become—a double-edged sword—helpful when trying to locate Levin, not as useful when trying to get away with murder.

My parents are a sore subject. I chew at a hangnail. I'm restless. This flight's short, less than an hour. Too much time to think.

Mom and Dad wanted me to go to therapy. They said they

were concerned for my well-being, but I think they were more worried about their safety.

After I left Oklahoma, I went directly to grad school to forget. I headed home afterward. Home was San Diego. Heidi took a toll on them, hell, she took a toll on me.

I'm sure they loved me in their own way, but they kept trying to dictate my life. They even had tried to warn Eric that I was unstable and host an intervention. They almost ruined the business before it was up and running.

That was an unforgivable sin.

Eric came to me after they spoke with him, the look of horror and concern in his voice as he shared with me what they had said.

"Bro, your parents are worried sick. They told me you went off your meds. Is this true?" Eric's voice was hushed. "I didn't know you were taking meds."

"I'm fine." I smoothed the annoyance in my voice over with a grin. "My parents don't know what they're talking about. They haven't seen me in years."

That part was true. I hadn't seen my parents in over two years since my senior year of college, since the accident. I hadn't meant to choke her to death. I just wanted to talk about the rumors I heard around campus—her impregnated with someone else's baby other than mine. I close my eyes as the image of her purplish, mottled face comes into view. How her eyes went lifeless, the color bleeding out of them, her heart eventually stopping. The baby. No more kicking in her belly.

Strike one.

Then they tried to get me committed.

Strike two.

That didn't work, so they decided to move to Florida.

Strike three.

When their car crashed into a concrete barricade, I felt a deep sadness that penetrated every fiber of my being.

They deserved it.

I couldn't trust Heidi not to fuck around.

I couldn't count on my parents to be supportive.

And now Levin. She left without my permission. And she would have to pay for that. No one left me. No one.

CHAPTER ELEVEN

LEVIN

I WAKE UP AFTER A RESTLESS SLEEP THE NEXT MORNING—one filled with flashbacks of my childhood and images of Alec chopping me into pieces.

I decide to wait to shower at the vacation rental. This place gives me the creeps—there's noise at all hours of the night and morning, people having sex and making animalistic noises and music echoing through the paper-thin walls. The peeling wallpaper doesn't offer any sound protection.

My skin is crawling from the itchy bed, and I ache. My neck and back are sore from the drive, and I'm jumpy but tired—an unpleasant combo.

I find my way to the other side of town—the houses start to appear better kept, the ailing stucco is replaced by updated versions, and the small, unkempt yards give way to larger parcels with the distinct touch of a gardener and landscaper.

Coffee is a must, and I pick one up as I head to the vacation rental.

As soon as I get to my second-floor condo, I decide to calm my nerves down with a glass of wine. No judgment on the fact it's filled to the brim and midday.

I can barely hold it steady, my hands still shaking. I have the curtains up, and I stare out the window as I consume big gulps from the glass before I remind myself to slow down.

The condo is small compared to the mini-mansion I was living in but perfect for me. A place to live that is mine, away from Alec's watchful eye, is a relief.

My surroundings are sparse. The furniture is outdated and mismatched, but I love it nonetheless. There isn't much in the place—some furniture, dishes, and odds and ends—but it is located in what should be a great area for me.

I like that the flooring is tile and hardwood, and it is small and compact. There's only one bedroom, but it has a Jack and Jill bath, so the two entrances connect from the bedroom to the bath and also from the hallway.

I walk through the place lost in thought.

What a rough couple of days.

The desire to sleep is overtaking my body almost like I've let out a big sigh of relief and can breathe. Almost.

Until Alec is put away, I won't.

But sleep beckons me. I need it badly.

I turn on the TV trying to get lost in the mindless chatter of a daytime courtroom judge. I take deep breaths.

As I start to drift off to sleep, my body is rigid as my mind starts to wander back in time to the ever-changing line-up of my mother's boyfriends. After Jeff, there had been Hank.

In middle school, my mother started dating him. Hank loved motorcycles and biker bars, so my mom started dressing in leather vests and ripped jeans. They would travel around on his Harley and leave me at home for periods of time. I was twelve. I didn't mind so much since that meant no one was around to bother me. The problem was that they often forgot to leave me money. There would be an empty refrigerator and bare cupboards, and my mom didn't have a cell phone then.

Eric and I first bonded over the fact that neither of our parents were around. His dad was always traveling for work, and his mom usually went with him. They felt like Eric was old enough to man the house, and there was a nanny who lived on the property, so they didn't feel like they were leaving him to his own devices.

At that moment, the doorbell rings. I freeze, petrified.

There's a kitchen knife in the top drawer. I grab it and walk slowly toward the door.

Who could be ringing my bell?

There is a small window with curtains near the entrance, but I didn't dare peek out. He couldn't have found me already, could he?

CHAPTER TWELVE

ALEC

WHEN I ARRIVE IN PHOENIX, I AM ALWAYS SURPRISED AT the weather. Even this late at night, it's still oppressive.

Just like Heidi. Just like my parents. Just like Eric.

All dictating to me how my life should go, all thinking they had a say in it.

Dry heat, my ass. I don't know how people survive here. I'd take California any day of the week. Luckily, it is fall, and temps are in the nineties during the day. I can handle this with air-conditioning and water. At least Levin hadn't chosen the middle of summer to leave.

My jaw clenches in anger as I think of all the trips we'd taken over the summer—Greece, Canada, Mexico, Bermuda, and Fiji. Of course, she enjoyed traveling the world on my dime.

Growing up, her family vacations had consisted of every state surrounding Nebraska. She might have been to a few state fairs and rodeos, but she had never seen culture or been privy to the best restaurants and shopping. I would think her, of all people, would want our children to be raised in an environment she could only dream of—a home and stability. I had given her that.

I decide to rent a large Chevy Suburban, the cargo space necessary if needed. A car would have been too small. You never know when you're going to have to transport something—or someone. I chuckle to myself, wishing I could let Levin in on the joke. It might make her re-think leaving.

There's a Plan B if Levin approached me about Eric's murder or didn't follow my instructions.

I crack my knuckles, the noise and the fact I do this out of annoyance always bothers Levin. I glare in the rearview mirror at my reflection. I would almost welcome her chastising me at this moment in time.

The SUV came with tinted windows that were black enough no one could see inside.

Maybe it was a blessing in disguise she headed to the valley of sunshine. At least tinting windows didn't raise suspicions or result in tickets like they did in other states.

You would think sleep would be imminent, but I'm unglued, mentally and physically with racing thoughts, jittery like I drank an entire pot of coffee. There's no point in attempting sleep.

I decide to drive around, aimless at first, but then with a sense of purpose. I should get a handle on the area and at least know certain landmarks—closest gas station, home improvement store, landfill.

CHAPTER THIRTEEN

LEVIN

GLANCING THROUGH THE PEEPHOLE, I SEE AN ELDERLY woman with a small mixed-breed dog at my door.

I inch the door open slowly.

"You must be my new neighbor," she exclaims. She's tall and wiry wearing a pink and white-striped tracksuit and orange sneakers.

I step outside onto the concrete and close the door behind me.

"Hi." I'm shy in the face of a new neighbor and potentially someone who could give me away. "Who's this cutie?" I kneel down to pet the bouncing bronco of a dog jumping all over.

"Harvey," she says. "He's a poodle mix I got from the pound a few years ago."

"Cute." I rub his soft fur.

"I'm Elsie Bancroft if you need anything." She waves to her condo.

"Levin," I say, shaking her hand. We make small talk for a minute, and then I head back inside the condo.

I call Maddy, and she answers on the first ring.

"I'm here," I say.

"Thank God." She is relieved. "I was telling Doug that I better get a call from you soon or I'm putting out an APB!"

"I stayed in a crappy hotel last night, but now I'm at the place." I didn't want to go into too much detail over the phone.

"Your trainer is asking where you went." She laughs. "He doesn't care about anyone else but you."

"Oh, no, I hope he doesn't call Alec. He'll assume we're sleeping together."

"I didn't say a word. I said I had no idea where you were." She pauses. "For all we know, you are living the lap of luxury with a stud you met on one of those dating sites."

"*Farmers Only*," I volunteer.

We both laugh.

Maddy's tone takes on a serious note. "Let me know what you need to settle in."

"I appreciate it. I'm going to run and get some groceries." I tap my foot, the sneaker thudding on the floor, the list of errands growing. "Then I'll call Amada. I start work tomorrow with her."

Amada is her cousin and my lifeline here.

Maddy is worried. "I just want you to be safe. Are you sure we can't just heave Alec off a bridge?" She is kidding, but I know she just wants what is best for me.

I laugh. "Nah, he is too narcissistic to jump."

"Well, holler if you need me. If you go more than twenty-four hours without a call, I'm going to find you." Maddy is struggling to control her emotions. "I am so scared, Levin."

On edge, I nod into the phone constantly checking to

make sure the door is locked, and no one is peeking through the windows.

"I know." I am quiet, pensive. "I will be careful. Tomorrow I'll be with your cousin."

"Thank goodness." I hear kids screaming in the background. "Okay, doll, talk soon. Call me anytime, you hear?"

I smile into the phone. Yes. I think to myself, yes, I will.

Because I moved around a lot as a kid and was ashamed of where I lived, I didn't build trust or focus on friends.

Bringing people over to the house was a no-no, first because of the fighting between my parents, then with Jeff and the unwanted and lecherous looks. Next up, who wants to give the grand tour of an eight hundred square foot trailer? Please make yourself at home, the bathroom sink doubles as the kitchen one, I think wryly.

Madison aka 'Maddy' Ferguson is different. I met her at the gym when I dropped a weight, all fifteen pounds punishing my left foot. I was hobbling around in pain, and she came to my rescue—her voice soothing, the 'mom' tone in place. She is maternal and savvy and thoughtful, helping me sit, ice my foot, and telling me hilarious stories about other gym patrons to make me laugh. The best one is the man who wears a banana hammock to lift weights—his veins not the only thing popping out.

It doesn't take long for Maddy and me to bond at the gym café or attend a Barre class together. Her schedule is prohibitive, as she has a couple of children and a husband to manage, but she always makes time for working out and our conversations.

I glance out the window checking the surroundings. I watch as a man jogs on the walking path outside, full speed ahead.

It's hardly a time-crunch as I unpack my minimal belongings. The place is sparse but comfortable.

In the bottom of a cardboard box I brought is a tattered copy of the book, *Are You There God, It's Me Margaret* by Judy Blume.

The book brings tears to my eyes. It is Eric's and my favorite childhood author, and this particular book was a gift from him to me. The value of this is monumental but not monetary—the significance is in the pages as ripped as they are.

I could never give away the book even though every year my mom had held a garage sale in hopes of paying our rent when she got behind. Other trinkets and toys would be sold, but this book was off-limits.

One year she had put it in a bin to discard it, and I had flipped out slamming doors and threatening to run away. Since then, the book had been in Eric's possession, and it had moved with him to his dorm room, our apartment senior year, and then eventually, to his loft. It was our spot for slipping letters and confidences to each other away from the curious eyes of our significant others, though I rarely had one long enough even to invite them over or introduce them. The women he brought home were also disposed of quite quickly as they seemed to realize along the way that he wasn't going to love them the way they needed or deserved. But through our rocky relationships with others, he remained the glue that held us together. He was mine—all I had in the world—losing him had cost me a great deal.

The book belongs on a shelf, a talisman that makes me feel Eric's energy.

Has Alec ever loved anything enough not to destroy it? Did killing someone give him a thrill? His tagline in business, 'the thrill of the kill,' seems like a double entendre to me.

My hands tremble as I set the book on the desk, a disturbing thought as his motto takes on new meaning. If he's capable of killing Heidi and Eric, two of the closest people in his life, then there is no doubt that I'm a target.

I have a bullseye on my back and a stabbing pain in my heart.

CHAPTER FOURTEEN

ALEC

I DON'T WANT TO DRAW ATTENTION TO MYSELF AND HAD chosen a non-descript hotel chain that accepted cash payments and didn't ask for a credit card.

It goes without saying, it's a pay-by-the-hour joint, but one can't be too picky when they're in the game of kidnapping.

The cash deposit I hand over to the front desk clerk is for more than the room, it's for my peace of mind. I don't want to be bothered. Stay the fuck out of my room. And my way.

They're more than willing to cater to my needs, a tip unnecessary but appreciated, the front desk manager offers. I explain to him... wink, wink... that I have a girlfriend visiting. No more questions are needed. No more answers are given. The front desk manager is an overweight, bald, sleazy man, and he likes the fact I allude to my rendezvous. He's in awe that I have both a wife and mistress, and I am happy to humor him when he suggests we grab a beer sometime. I might need his help. Best to keep him intrigued.

I would assume Levin had planned to stay at an expensive resort, more her style than a Super 8, but a search of her email tells a different story. Levin must've rented an apartment or condo. I search through her sent emails and find a plethora of rentals she has inquired about in the past. She is prone to seasonal depression so it makes sense she would prefer sunshine and mountains over the other states.

Unless there is someone else. A reason to come here.

In her email, I find just what I'm looking for. She has transferred money to a lady named Cheryl Bradley. There's a PayPal email that shows a money transfer a month ago. I clench my fists. A month ago, my future bride decided to leave me. The one Levin ends up renting is a short-term lease and consists of a one bedroom, second floor unit in the south end of Scottsdale. The deposit and two months' rent is required up front and paid. I am furious that I missed this email. She had deleted it out of her 'sent' mail. I found it in the spam cache.

Of course, I knew she wasn't going anywhere. I would let her have a few days to cool off, to think I have given her space and start to feel like she could start a new life without me. Then I would pounce.

I think about the baby we are going to have.

Her absentee parents.

She and I would be devoted to our children. With the money from Eric's inheritance, she could be a stay-at-home mom. Didn't she realize what she was being given? The opportunity to raise children and get love and attention from not only me, but from them? This would make her childhood all worth the pain and would replace the abandonment she felt from her own family.

Couldn't she see this was just as much for her as it was for me?

It is in her best interest to marry me and conceive my children.

Our children, I suppose I should say.

A therapist told me I use 'I' instead of 'we' too much, and that I have illusions of grandeur. I inflate my self-importance.

I crack my knuckles. What is the point of paying someone to put you down? This is why I don't believe in therapy. No one should get paid to label you.

That therapist. Well, I didn't see her again. After that last unfortunate accident.

She fell down some stairs. I waited until after her last client for the evening and hid in the doorway of the office suite next to hers.

My smiles are terse as I think of the sound the baseball bat made as it connected with her knee, which made her crumble down the stairs.

Tonya Harding style.

Wasn't a bad idea. Thanks to the Olympic Trials for that idea.

Levin isn't getting any younger. I am her only hope for marriage and a family. At least that's what I tell myself. The only other person who cared about Levin as I do is gone. Such a shame that Eric decided to take the easy way out.

He didn't technically have a choice, I made it for him, even wrapping the noose around his neck and pushing his feet off the chair.

I don't want to have to make Levin's choice for her, but I will.

I'll start by giving her some space.

I decide I'm not going to contact her.

She won't know what to do when I don't show I am chasing her. No phone calls, emails, or texts to her.

This man... if it is a man she left me for, I want to see him. He probably tried to woo her, tell her she would love the desert and promised her a good life. Why, then, is she living in a shithole condo?

If Levin thought her lifestyle would come with her, she is batshit crazy. I made her who she is today. If another man thought I was going to give her up easily after all I had invested in her over the past year, he was crazy.

Crazier, even than me.

CHAPTER FIFTEEN

LEVIN

ON WEDNESDAY, I REPORTED FOR DUTY, PUNCTUALITY A must—7:00 a.m. on the dot.

A staff meeting consisted of myself and the other four household helpers who would be taking care of the guests. The boss was a woman named Olivia Martinez, a thick, Hispanic woman who wore her black hair in a tight bun.

"Levin Crowdley?" My name pierced through the room as she called my name.

"Here." I swallowed my gum and raised my hand.

"Great, nice to meet you." Her smile revealed a gap between her two front teeth. "I have assigned you to four rooms, and from your resume and Amada, it looks like you're quite the addition to the team." Amada was Maddy's cousin, and she sat to my left.

Amada and I smiled at each other. Maddy had not given her my entire sordid history, but she knew I was in dire need of a job.

She handed us all a sheet of paper with the villa name and the registered guest's information. Dietary restrictions and their favorite foods were listed along with the clothing and shoe sizes and a snapshot of their lifestyles. It was a miniature bible on every client that was staying at the Triple T as they called it.

From my list of guests, one was a recently married couple celebrating their honeymoon, another was a woman who was a keynote speaker at a civil engineering conference—no small feat I imagined—one was an old man who had recently been widowed, and the other was a man in his mid-forties and the CEO of a solar energy company.

We went around and introduced ourselves. Lupita and Angela were the other two in addition to Amada and me. Lupita looked to be pushing forty and spoke little English. She had long, dark hair that reached her butt, and she kept it pushed off her face in a hair clip. Angela looked younger than her years—she could have passed for a high schooler as she barely made the five-foot mark. She was petite and had golden hair, bright blue eyes, and translucent skin. She was a high school dropout and seemed to use 'like' after every other word. Amada reminded me of Maddy—they shared the same laugh and some of the same mannerisms both picking their nails and playing with their hair. Amada also had the same body type as Maddy. I could have picked her out of a crowd anywhere.

My first day on the job was getting acquainted with the property and checking on my 'clients,' as we called them. I spent the rest of my afternoon trying to take my mind off Alec. As I ran errands for the married couple, I couldn't help but wonder why they had decided to get married. What was it about people that made them want to commit to someone else?

When my mom died of lung cancer at the ripe age of

forty-seven, I thought I had seen it all. She had been a smoker since she was fifteen, and her boyfriends either puffed on cigarettes or imbibed in harder drugs. I had taken care of her for the last few years of her life.

The hours pass in a blur. It is a good distraction from the turn my life has taken, a rat race now instead of the straight and narrow.

I spend my hours running errands for the various villas. The irony of switching places in life isn't lost on me. I grew up poor, then did a switcharoo and hired the help—the chef and the trainer and the maids. Now I'm back to waiting hand and foot on people, some more appreciative than others. There are those who are born rich with all the opportunities life affords them and never have to struggle. I envy them at times, but also feel sorry for them, to never understand what it is like to count the days until payday as your bank account dwindles or to know what it is like to have Christmas on layaway.

Most of these tasks are ones Alec refused to do for himself or allow me to do.

There's dry-cleaning to pick up, a couple of suits that need custom tailoring, and multiple drop-offs and pick-ups.

One woman asks for a spa manicure and pedicure kit since she didn't have time to run to the nail salon. Another wanted some magazines, so I made a stop at Target for some reading materials. Anything they wanted, they felt like they could ask for.

In the afternoon, I helped one client with her wardrobe selections. It was a busy day, and it wasn't long before my thoughts drifted off to what I was going to do here. How long could I stay before it was apparent I was being hunted?

I knew Alec wouldn't just accept that I was gone. He wasn't used to people leaving him.

I dog walked one of the client's Dalmatians that came

along to the resort wondering if he is a guard dog and can attack on demand.

Olivia needed my help in the office in the afternoon with some spreadsheets, so I happily obliged. Anything to keep my mind off the personal vendetta Alec Durant would have against me.

CHAPTER SIXTEEN

ALEC

I'M PACING IN MY ROOM WEARING A HOLE IN THE CARPET, edgy as I think about what she's doing.

Fuck it, I think. I know George is handling the situation and is capable, but I decide to take matters into my own hands.

I drive to where the rental is located and park myself in a corner of the parking lot, an unassigned spot close enough to where she would enter the building but far enough away that she would not look straight into the vehicle. I'm in the black Suburban, so I know she won't spot me even if she comes outside.

If there's a man who brought her here, I want to know.

What if she's pregnant? She's been tired lately, pushing me away when I try to be intimate. She cringes at my touch.

It might be better than her knowing about my past.

I almost feel ashamed that I haven't asked. It has been months since we became engaged, and she has stopped taking the pill. Maybe she freaked out because she was scared, maybe she felt alone, or like I didn't care? I have been working an awful lot to try to stop the siphoning of money from the business account.

It keeps dwindling especially now that Eric isn't around to fill the coffers. Business has slowed down, and Eric had helped with bringing in a lot of our newest land development clients. A lot of my time was devoted to investing in our future trying to make money.

Let's just say managing our funds wasn't my strong suit. I like to gamble in life—real estate and online poker—and sometimes you go in the negative. Eric didn't appreciate my zest for taking blind leaps.

I'm a likeable guy, always the life of the party, and I know I'm convincing. I tried to rationalize my spending with him. He wasn't buying my reasons. Or excuses.

Eric warned me about spending *his* money, the time I spent online, the risks I took. If

only he knew the biggest risk I made—asking Levin to marry me and start a new life with her.

If Levin's pregnant, she needed me more than ever. Maybe she didn't move here to start over with another man. Maybe she moved here to get away from me.

I couldn't think of any friends in Phoenix. I go through her *Facebook* friends one by one to verify there aren't any Phoenix connections. It's time-consuming but crucial.

It's all a mystery to me, but a mystery that would be unraveled shortly.

My breath comes out in short spurts. I'm almost relieved that I might've solved the mystery of why she left. I imagine poor Levin alone with our baby in a new city.

With a renewed sense of purpose, I sit and wait—wait for the love of my life, and possibly, the loves of my life, to come back. After all, life is all about waiting. Waiting for what you want. I would sit and wait. But only for a little while.

I head to a local Home Depot and put on a ball cap and sunglasses. I don't want anyone seeing my face or eyes. I'm low-key wearing sweatpants which are almost an embarrassment, my belly hanging over the waistband. A baggy t-shirt covers most of my mid-section. I can't remember the last time I dressed down like this. My attire consists of three-piece suits on most days or the color black slimming my small gut. Dressing down for me meant slacks and a golf tee.

Rope and duct tape is needed. A clerk offers to help me, but I decline his invite, his eyes follow me as I pretend to scrutinize paint samples, judging my color palette as I focus intensely on the color yellow.

I glance at a row of cleaning supplies and grab some cloth rags. I purchase some bleach and a mop, so it doesn't look as suspicious.

The moving boxes can be used to help Levin move her items back home.

Or they could have a dual purpose. I tug at my earlobe, the thought of her tiny body cramped and stuffed in the cheap cardboard box if she's problematic.

I'm not enthusiastic about rejection, especially from women who hold the purse strings. I'm in an impossible situation, and the loss of control is eating at me.

She's been acting off, and I imagine there's more to her attitude than just hormones. That's on her. I will find out soon enough.

One last item is the bungee cord. I hum as I make my way to the front, my mood slightly on the uptick as I push the cart to the checkout counter. The thought of Levin tied up is enough to make my body react favorably, her sprawled out in front of me, my little puppet.

I make sure to pay in cash, no paper trail, and the receipt is promptly chucked into the trash on the way out.

There's a place I rented here, a secluded house, a place where Levin and I can relax and re-group. Some R & R is a welcome distraction and much needed for the both of us.

Fate brought me together with Levin. She can try and cheat destiny all she wants, yet she can't avoid my plans for her. It's all coming to fruition, the groundwork already laid.

Now I just need to get my hands on my M.I.A. fiancée.

CHAPTER SEVENTEEN

Levin

As scatterbrained as I am today, I manage to help Olivia with the Excel spreadsheet that's giving her a headache.

The numbers blur, but I force myself to focus drowning out the thought of Alec strangling me to death, the same way he killed both Heidi and Eric.

After I finish, I'm relieved to take a walk and clear my head. The fresh air helps, but my mind is buried in this scenario—an image of Alec behind me, holding on to me for dear life—that I almost lose my balance, narrowly missing Villa 19's patron.

The CEO of the solar energy company, Jake Hunter, is Villa 19.

He's smoldering, all man—tall, muscular, a short-sleeved polo shirt hugging his biceps and dress pants slung low on his hips enveloping his slim waist.

I meet him as he's headed out of his villa, Ray-Bans

covering his eyes, brown leather briefcase in hand, Rolex on his wrist.

I stumble off the concrete walkway, the thought of being reunited with Alec a harsh reality, and almost barrel into Jake.

I'm relieved to be wearing Converse sneakers and not heels as I would've toppled over into the bushes. My face burns red, flustered as I bite my lip.

Such a klutz, my mother used to tell me. She was right about one thing.

Jake has a knee-jerk reaction and reaches out an arm, righting me. His strong arm is firm around my elbow. I mumble my thanks as he removes his sunglasses and sets down his briefcase. I introduce myself, feeling self-conscious in my short skirt and my graceless behavior.

He doesn't let go, and I'm facing the man whose life I'm supposed to help manage, yet I haven't mastered walking.

"Hi, Mr. Hunter, I'm Levin, your household helper," I say, fingering the hem of my skirt, wishing I had tumbled into the bushes and been swallowed whole avoiding this debacle.

There's a moment of silence as he looks at me, giving me a chance to catch my breath. There's confusion on his face as he contemplates my title, his head tilting slightly.

He glances at me, amused. "Household helper?"

"Basically, I'm your personal assistant." I have the urge to run but don't want to draw more attention to myself. Something about Jake is unsettling. It's more than his impossibly good looks.

The realization he's still holding my elbow dawns on him, and he drops it, letting his arm fall back to his side. "A personal assistant, huh?" He whistles in appreciation, grinning at me.

"Jake." He reaches out and shakes my hand, the silver metal of his watch glinting in the sunlight. Since he took his sunglasses off, it's impossible not to notice the flecks of gold in them. "You can call me Jake."

I nod. "Okay, Mr. Hunter, I mean, Jake." I'm trying not to notice the way his six-foot-tall frame towers over me.

"Before you go, I just want to make sure..." I ramble on. "Are there any foods you don't like? What's your favorite drink?" The list of questions makes me dizzy, but I want to do a good job and to do that, I need to be thorough. "Do you like wine or no? Any certain types?"

"I like vodka-based drinks. Think vodka soda with a twist of lime. Usually Tito's." He stares at me, his liquid-gold eyes narrow. "I like white wine, but I'll drink red depending on the mood." With that, he gives me a flirtatious wink.

I smile. I hope he's my most easy-going client. "What about food preferences?"

"I don't like peas." He's solemn as he says this. "I also don't like cabbage or pastrami on rye or anything that tastes like lamb."

I make mental notes as he adds, "I'm not a vegetarian."

"Duly noted."

"What, exactly, does a PA do?" His eyebrows knit together in curiosity.

"Errands. Dry cleaning. Shopping. Stocking your room with food requests." I tick them off on my fingers as I list them off. "If you call me at 5:00 a.m. and need Band-Aids and Alka-Seltzer, I'm your gal."

"Five-star service." He purses his lips in thought. "I might need your help with shopping."

"That, I can do." I rest my hand on my hip, staring at him, the idea of picking out his clothes or shopping for him a daunting task. What if he hates what I pick out? I always considered myself to have chic taste, but Alec told me I had no sense of style. Worse yet, what if it's shopping for a wife or girlfriend?

I glance down to check if there's a ring. Nada. Which means nothing. Maybe he's engaged?

"I also might need your help on restaurant choices." He motions with his hands. "I have a place here, but it's being rented out, and my other home's in the middle of renovations. Though I spend a decent amount of time here for work, I need some new go-to places."

"Of course." I tuck a loose strand of hair behind my ear. "I'll do some checking on *Yelp* and *OpenTable* and see what I can find."

"Are you a transplant or a native?" He's taken a slight step forward, and I want to move back, the idea of him in my space makes me nervous. Not in a bad way, but there's an energy I feel in his presence, and I'm trembling, my palms shaking as I try to hide them by my side.

"No, I grew up in another state." I give him a small smile, "Most recently lived in San Diego."

"Best weather." He smiles at me, searching my face. I hold his stare before I glance down at the ground pretending to notice my shoelace is untied.

I lean down to re-tie my lace, take a breath, and stand back up.

This gives him the opportunity to take a glimpse at his watch. "Crap." He looks at the time. "I gotta run, I'm gonna be late for the meeting I'm hosting." He laughs, and the crease lines near his eyes crinkle. He's the perfect specimen of a man.

I shake my head in understanding.

"So nice to meet you, Levin." He touches my arm for a brief second. I might've imagined it lingers there longer than necessary. "I'm sure I'll be seeing more of you than you'd like."

I laugh as he says, "I'll try not to be the annoying one, that 'one guy' who's the topic of all your convos here." He pushes his shades down and strolls off, briefcase in hand, exuding an aura of confidence. I sigh as I remember that's what I thought about Alec when I met him—his brashness a turn-on unlike my father's weak backbone in life. Though his aplomb reminds me of Alec, he has a different essence—the ability to laugh at oneself, find humor in situations.

Jake Hunter's a head honcho, but there's a quality about him that I'm attracted to. Magnanimous.

Alec has an underlying tone—it manifests itself in anger—controlled, but manifests in his emotions or his body language. He's a bully. And a killer.

He can be brilliant but destructive. I fell in love with him but saw that his charm is forced. He's selfish and egotistical to a fault. When you first fall in love, you ignore the negative, even though they flash like a neon sign in front of your face. I jumped in headfirst, seeing only the best. Now I'm prepared for the worst.

CHAPTER EIGHTEEN

Alec

I wake up to the sound of a car horn beeping.

Disoriented, I rub my eyes. I passed out in the Suburban, not even staying awake to see if Levin came or went.

This is why I need a PI. There are some chores I can't do on my own.

Multiple missed calls are flashing on my phone.

George.

I pound the redial button and rub a hand over my face in frustration. I'm not patient. If I had my way, I'd grab Levin and drag her ass to the rental house.

The business is going to go under if I don't get a commission check soon.

"Where the hell are you?" I'm cranky from sleeping in a cramped position. I rub my neck as he ignores my tone. "I need her back *now,*" I hiss.

"AJ's on 5th Street in Old Town," he says and hangs up.

A quick *Google* search shows it's a dive bar not far from

the vacation rental. I drive past it once, missing the obtuse lettering. 'AJ's' is on a wooden, faded, nondescript sign out front.

I pull into a parking space in front of an old and decrepit bar that reminds me of where I spent my college years. George is waiting in the parking lot, kicking at the curb in his worn-in cowboy boots.

According to George, the best Moscow Mules were served here. I'm willing to take him up on his suggestion to try one considering my mood.

I'm contemplative, the thought of Levin and how she calls Moscow Mules 'Moscow Meows' and then does a cat impression. I laugh to myself. George looks startled, and I just shake my head 'no.' There's no explanation needed. He gets I'm a bit off at times.

The fact that this place is not based on appearances is appealing to me at this moment in time.

I step on something sticky on the ground and wrinkle my nose. Maybe not.

We walk inside, and though it's fairly dark, they have an enclosed patio that absorbs lots of natural light. George heads to the bar and orders two Moscow Mules while I find us a table. Usually, we avoid being seen in public together, but this place has a light crowd because of the hour. The happy-hour crowd hasn't come in yet.

Within minutes, he brings the cold copper mugs back to the table and sits down. He hands me one and says, "Cheers."

I roll my eyes but manage to echo back a 'Cheers' while tapping my mug against his.

"Levin," he says her name, getting down to business. He knows I don't like to mince words.

"Yes," I swallow a sip of the Mule, but I don't taste it.

"She's working at a resort. Started today, I'm going to

check it out tomorrow." George takes a swig and grabs a notepad out of his shirt pocket.

I purse my lips as he says this. "A *resort?*" I'm incredulous. I can imagine Levin interior decorating or working with various charities but not in the hospitality business waiting on others. The life I gave her ensured that others waited on her, not vice-versa.

My temper's starting to rise, my composure slipping away. I grip the table, the wood cutting into my fingers. "There's someone else," I spit out, "... isn't there?"

George shakes his nod in disagreement. "You're jumping to conclusions."

"I doubt she would give up our life for being nothing more than a servant." Resentment is boiling over. The fact she left me, and it came out of left field, a punch to my gut. I slam the rest of the drink, the vodka and ginger beer sliding down my throat.

George squints at me and abruptly changes the subject. My slanted eyes a sign that I'm incapable of anything more than wallowing in my misery at this point.

"Any of her family still alive?" George is poised and all business. "I couldn't find any but wanted to confirm."

I shake my head no. "Her parents are dead. Dad died of cirrhosis and Mom died of cancer—lung cancer." I quietly wring my hands underneath the table. "They weren't together when they passed. They got divorced when she was young, then a bad string of relationships." I remember the story Eric told me about meeting Levin for the first time.

Though they didn't live far from each other, it might as well have been two different counties, the way he described it.

Eric grew up in a gated community in a huge, brick house that backed up to a pond on an acre of land. She lived in a trailer with her mom and her mom's latest squeeze. She and

Eric met when he was riding his bike, and she was walking up the street to a gas station to ask for a job. The story goes that he almost ran her down pedaling through a stop sign.

That's the story of how they met, both yearning for a friend.

My face goes from dark to light and then dark again, lost in my troubled thoughts. A negative image replaced by a happy one. I picture the two of them together and know if Eric were still in the picture, there would have been no room for the three of us.

George finishes his drink, silent, both of us immersed in our own ominous, frenzied emotions.

"You thinking about your wife?" I tease, trying to lighten the mood.

"No, I'm not." George is serious. "What about you? You still want to get married to her?"

"Yeah. I motion to the bartender for another Mule. "You want a second one?"

"Sure." He nods.

"I came close a couple of times. I dated a girl seriously in college, and I thought she was the one." I put my hands behind my head and lean back in the chair. "Then I dated another woman for a few years, but it didn't work out." I shrug. "Think she lives in New Mexico now."

It goes from dead to alive as a crowd of people starts to fill the bar. It is a younger group, twenty-somethings that just got off of work, the ones who live for happy hour because of the cheap liquor. They're excited, a sense of merriment in the air. The sticky floor and the broken stools don't bother them —this is what they live for after graduating college and entering the real world. It's a sense of pride being able to pull out their wad of bills, buy their friends a beer, impress the girl next to them.

They order appetizers and drinks around us, but we aren't

concerned with them. The mugs sweat, the condensation sliding its way down the smooth sides. I wish I'm in bed with Levin, my hands moving down her body soaking her in.

I exhale, feeling another jab to my insides. The jagged edges of my memory are retreating into the past.

This must be what love feels like. Crazy, because I thought I loved Heidi, thought I loved my parents, and I thought I loved Eric like a brother.

Heidi was a sweet girl at the beginning of our courtship. She didn't like that I challenged her. Emotional abuse, she called it. She said her therapist told her that I wasn't the right caliber for her.

That's when I went for my benefit to see what this woman who didn't know me had to say about me when she met me. I couldn't tell her I was Heidi's boyfriend.

I tried the therapy and the medications she prescribed for my depression for a while. I gave her a shot expressing my concerns about my girlfriend. She never put it together, that she was treating both of us.

It became too much when she diagnosed me with a narcissistic personality disorder. A treatment of psychotherapy is the only way to cope, she said. It would take years of therapy to try and build up these fragile relationships. A collaboration between us was necessary, she explained.

I hated her. I loved Heidi, but I hated her. The way her mouth moved when she discussed me like I wasn't sitting ten fucking feet from her. Her coldness toward me was tantamount to her ugly stares and continuation of therapy.

But Levin. She cuts me deeper like a knife. She called me on bullshit most could never get away with.

The idea of a sharp knife makes me tingle, and I shiver involuntarily. I hoped I didn't have to demonstrate the kind of pain I was feeling on her body.

I stumble out of the bar having drunk my feelings. The night is starting to turn into a witching hour.

Mules turn into whiskey and turn into a go at the jukebox. Levin's and my favorite country song—the Kenny Chesney and Grace Potter ballad about tequila—gets me fired up. I almost drop a shot glass on the floor as I crumble my fist around the cool rim.

I'm envious of a young man at the bar hitting on the cute waitress, a blonde chick barely out of college—tiny frame and big boobs. She already has had a round of lip injections, and her fake lashes flutter as she flirts with him, eye fucking the shit out of him.

He's probably thirty, one of the better-looking boy scouts here. His jeans are ripped but fashionably showing tan skin over his kneecaps, and his tight muscle shirt clings to his six-pack.

Maybe I need to get some work done. Is Levin not attracted to me? I thought I had a decent body, maybe a little soft in spots, but I think it's pretty decent. I've had to go up a couple of pant sizes since I met her, but what's the big deal? Yes, it's not as agile or tight as it was in college, but I'm in decent shape. She's lucky to have a man who's focused on fitness and healthy eating.

I glance at myself in a mirror that hangs from the wall. It advertises beer, but I can see my appearance in the choppy reflection. I turn my profile looking at all sides.

I've seen some of the frumpy men looking like life beat them up and left them to putter along in baggy jeans and a Hawaiian shirt, unsure why they can't fuck their wives, let alone the wait staff. They're the same type of men who think strippers like them and want to go home with them.

Whereas I'm now unhinged, George is unaffected. His demeanor is the same—calm and collected. He drives me back to my hotel as I lean back against the headrest, the world spinning on its axis. How did everything tilt so out of whack?

I need Levin back.

The feeling of suffocation is constricting my airway. If I don't choke to death on my feelings tonight, Levin is going to feel the wrath.

Is this how Heidi and Eric felt when the air was sucked out of their lungs—one with my bare hands and one with rope—the tight grip expelling their last breath until their hyoid bone snaps?

They both had the same expression on their faces—bulging eyes and a sense of fear which reflected in their dilated pupils. Both wanted me to stop. They begged for their lives. I'm not going to lie, I enjoyed the attention, the promises of what they would do if I didn't let them die.

Death: I have always loved the word. The sense of finality. Some see it as an entrance to another side—dark or light—depending on your belief system. I see it as the end. No more pain from those that caused me suffering.

Heidi aborted a baby. She deserved to die. She killed a child so she could act like one. She also cheated. An unforgivable sin if you ask me.

Eric got greedy and self-serving. He caused the dissolution of a marriage and ruined innocent children's lives.

My parents had their flaws. If they had saved and been successful, money wouldn't have been an issue. When they died, I thought there would be more money. I was disgusted to find out they had nothing. I got the proceeds from the house. It was gone in a couple of months.

George can't help me to my room. It will draw unwanted attention to us. He parks in the lot at the hotel and waits for me to get my bearings. He shoves four aspirin in my palm as I wobble out of the vehicle.

I pass out in bed, fully clothed, as I sniff the arm of my

shirt and get a whiff of cigarette smoke. I smell like an ashtray and hard alcohol.

My dreams become nightmares as images of Levin in bed with the douche at the bar appear in my head. Her face is intermingled with the blonde waitresses, both oohing and aahing over his sic body.

I vaguely remember punching my pillow in exasperation when I wake up.

Then I black out. The night's decisions reflected in its consequences.

CHAPTER NINETEEN

LEVIN

ON MY SECOND DAY AT THE RESORT, A VEHICLE FOLLOWS ME out of the parking lot. I check my rearview mirror, my heart speeding up as the adrenaline rushes through my body. I try to ignore the pounding in my chest, and I grip the steering wheel.

I would know that cocky grin and that jet-black hair anywhere. It wasn't Alec, though. As I peer in my side mirror, I see a shock of salt and pepper hair, mostly salt, and tan, wrinkled skin. I need to call Maddy to talk me off a ledge as I can barely breathe, the rising panic starting to overwhelm me. I need to pull over.

The man's starting to slow behind me inching his way to a crawl. I flash my lights indicating he should go around me. He doesn't. At this pace, a turtle could pass both my car and his. I turn my four-way flashers on and pull over on the shoulder. This area is populated and in the middle of the city, so I don't feel vulnerable. I need to get a handle on my emotions.

I put my head on the steering wheel and rest it there for a minute, the cool plastic soothing my forehead.

I hear a knock on my driver-side window. The man from the car behind me stands there, all five-feet-eight inches of him, and his round belly is covered in a western plaid print as his hands hook on his oversized belt buckle. I wait, half expecting to see his lasso pop up at any minute.

He motions for me to roll down my window. The last thing I want to do is open myself up to strangers. I pause. I decide to let him know I am okay, but only through the window. I turn the vehicle back on and press the window button. I only put it down an inch.

The man is chewing tobacco. I can see the way his mouth rolls it around and tucks it in his bottom lip.

"Are you all right, miss?" His voice is gruff but kind.

"Yes. I... I just needed some air." I take a deep breath. "I was having a panic attack."

He nods, eyes squinting. "Do you know your way around here?"

"You mean, am I a local?" I pause. "I'm just visiting relatives."

"I noticed you came from the resort. That's where I'm staying." He pokes his cowboy boot in the dirt. "Just thought I'd ask if you needed a ride back. Or an escort." His voice didn't match his clothing. It sounded rough, but there was no twang.

"No, I'm meeting some friends," I lie. "Thank you for stopping."

I roll my window up to give him the hint I am done talking, but he stares at me for a second too long.

It gives me the creeps. Goosebumps pop up on my skin, a sign that my body is in sync with my mind.

Then he turns and limps back to his car, a slight hitch in his gait.

He doesn't move, and I wait for what seems like an eternity. I don't want him behind me. The lights go on, and he pulls back onto the road.

I wait a minute. Then I follow suit.

Something about him is familiar. I can't put my finger on it, though.

The Cadillac turns left, and I turn right. Phew.

I drive until I hit a CVS Pharmacy and exit my vehicle. My sunglasses are on hiding the paranoia and redness from crying in the car.

Inside, I buy a water, a magazine, and minutes for my phone. I want to call Maddy.

When I leave the store, I notice the Caddy driving around the back entrance of the CVS. It is too far away to make out the driver, but I notice it is him. Arizona doesn't require front license plates, but his vehicle has Tennessee plates.

I tell myself this is a coincidence. Of course, it is. No one knows me here. He's an older man, senile.

He's not, though.

The two choices I have are to wait for him to notice me leaving the drugstore and follow me, or play a game of cat and mouse. I choose the latter.

I have about five seconds before he comes around the building again. I run to the car and hide in the backseat. I lay across the leather seats and hope he doesn't stop near my vehicle. There are cars on both sides of me so he can't park next to me.

My cell phone is next to me on the seat. I call Maddy. It rings and goes to voicemail. "Maddy, someone is following me," I say. "I'm at the CVS drug store off Scottsdale Road and um, Lincoln, I think. Will try you again later."

I start to inch up the glass giving me a reflection on all sides. He is making his way around the building again. I climb into the driver's seat from the back and wait, ducked down, for him to drive by again. I hear a commotion next to me and see a couple getting into the two-seater Lexus beside me. I am out of time. He will park beside me and will kill me. I wonder if Alec is here. I only saw one man in the car. Maybe Alec is waiting for me elsewhere.

My lunch is starting to rise in my throat, the bile making its way to the air. I am trying not to gag as I start the engine and back up. I gun it as soon as I am in a position to do so and tear off through the parking lot.

The silver Cadillac is coming around the corner. I manage to squeal out into traffic. He tries to pursue me but almost runs into a speeding pick-up truck.

I breathe a sigh of relief. With steady traffic, I can lose him.

The rental is my only safety net. There's no paper trail of me renting it, and it's not in my name. I need to ditch this car. There's an Enterprise down the street from the condo, and I head there. Checking my mirrors, I find no sign of a silver car, so I park the vehicle in the back of the Enterprise dealership out of sight from the main road.

"Hi," I say when I get up to the counter. "I need to switch cars. This one is making a funny noise."

"Really?" The clerk says, fingers tapping his computer keyboard. "Of course. Mid-size work?"

"Sure." I trade him my keys and get a black Hyundai Sonata. I use the credit card Maddy gave me along with her old ID that resembles me if you squint hard enough. He makes copies of both, and I show him my insurance card, a copy of Maddy's.

I check again to make sure there's no sign of Alec or the old man.

I'm safe.

For now.

The vacation condo is a few blocks away, and I pull into the parking lot, enter the gate code, and watch as the gates click shut behind me. They are a false sense of security. I know this. Something about them makes me feel safe, though, like a moat at a castle would. There's a detached garage, and I park inside carefully paying attention to my surroundings.

My heart is threatening to beat outside of my chest. I sit behind the steering wheel and focus on breathing short, shallow breaths to the count of ten.

If I go to the cops, will they believe me?

Liz wanted me to run, so I did.

Eric told me his truth, so I believe it.

The proof is the problem. I am scared of whom I can trust. Maddy wanted to go to the cops, and I had a meltdown. What if she ended up dead? Her kids now orphans because of my suspicions? Her husband left alone because of my actions.

Alec seems to infiltrate aspects of my life that he shouldn't. He knows intimate details that he shouldn't. Someone helps him. That much I know.

That man in the Caddy is familiar. I have seen him in San Diego. I'm flustered and can't put my finger on it now.

I pull out the card in my wallet. It is Janice Hendricks' Avon Consultant card. I dial and wait for it to ring. I am scared to leave the dark garage, for once, the blackness is a safety net. There are no windows in the space, and for all I know, the man could be outside, stalking his prey—in this case—me.

A voice answers. It is chipper.

"This is Janice with Avon."

"Janice," I stammer, "this is Levin. Levin Crowdley. I got your card from Liz."

There is a pause. I think the phone is disconnected.

"I thought you would never call." The voice is in shock on the other end.

I'm confused. "Was I not supposed to?"

"No, no, no, no." Janice is breathing hard. "Do you know who I am?"

"Liz's friend? Someone I can call to get in touch with Liz?" I lean my head against the glass on the driver's side.

"No, I mean, yes, I am Liz's friend," Janice says. "I know Liz because of Heidi."

There is silence for a moment. It is deafening.

"Levin, I used to be Heidi's roommate. I'm the one who found her." Janice continues, the words slamming into one another like a tsunami. "I found her dead."

I instantaneously feel the air go out of my lungs. I can't breathe. A panic attack overtakes me. I gasp for air, throw open the car door and heave myself on the concrete floor, my phone still grasped tight in my hand.

"Hello?" Janice voice echoes, her concern apparent. "Levin, are you there? Please don't hang up."

"Why would I hang up?" I mumble into the phone.

A loud sigh comes across the line. "I didn't know if we should tell you."

"What happened to Heidi?" I am hysterical. "What the hell happened to her? What did *he* do?"

Another long silence. "Janice, I'm being chased by someone, probably him or an accomplice. I want to go to the police, but he's always a step ahead. I need to know what I'm dealing with."

"Levin," she states my name like she is calling on me in class. "That was the worst night of my life..." She chokes up, "... and I relive it every day.

"I was out of town. My boyfriend attended a community college so I'd make the trek there or vice-versa. He was older and had his own apartment, so it was easier to be alone at his place. Heidi..." Janice stops mid-sentence. "God, I sound so selfish. It was so selfish only caring about *my* boyfriend.

"Heidi had found out she was pregnant. She had been seeing a guy named Brad. She and Alec had a complicated relationship, and they were always fighting. I was relieved when she took up with Brad. I thought it might persuade Alec to leave her alone. He never did. He would show up unannounced. This was before cell phones, so he would knock at all hours of the night or follow her to class. He was... is... nuts."

"Was she scared?" My voice is hollow.

"Yes, to both. Being pregnant and unmarried and because Alec stalked her." Janice is hoarse. "He couldn't get it through his head she didn't want him."

"Did her parents know?" I can only imagine how most moms would feel about their children's safety.

"She talked to her mom a lot, but it was like once a week. You have to remember, though, this is before the latest and greatest. Cell phones were just starting to become available, and there was no social media.

"I went with her to get the abortion. She was terrified, understandably. She talked about dropping out of school, but I encouraged her not to, to give it another semester."

"Did the baby's father know about the baby?"

"No," Janice says flatly. "That would've complicated things. Her situation wasn't as accepted as it is now."

"Did he know she was pregnant, Alec?" I ask.

"I don't know," she murmurs. "He very well could've. He stalked her and could have assumed from the clinic visit. It was confidential, but she was showing, and of course, she hadn't had her period for a while."

"Wouldn't he just assume it was his?"

"No, Heidi never slept with him."

I'm floored. "She didn't sleep with Alec, but she slept with Brad?"

"Bingo. She had planned to wait for the six-month mark with Alec. Brad was a fluke, she was drunk, and it happened." Janice is pensive. "Brad liked her and started walking her to class. They started dating, and it left a bad taste in Alec's mouth."

Janice's voice catches as she finishes the story. "It was fall break so a long weekend, and we had three days off. I came home Monday night to find our place ransacked. He made it look like a break-in, throwing papers around and breaking our computer. I was *so* scared to look through the rest of the place in case the intruder was still there. Something made me continue, made me check our bedrooms. Mine had my pillows and sheets thrown around, a lamp smashed. Nothing horrible.

"Hers... " Janice swallows hard, "... had her body in her bed. He had posed her naked, not even bothering to cover her up." The disgust is oozing out of her voice. "He broke her neck."

I am gasping for air, seated Indian style on the concrete, my back pushed up against the garage wall. I don't want to leave the garage, yet I dread staying here.

"Levin?" Janice sounds far away. "Are you okay, honey?"

"I'm so scared he's going to kill me." I sound so level-headed like I am discussing someone else.

"I've gotta call the police." Janice is firm. "Where are you?"

I shake my head as if she can hear me nod my head no through the phone.

"No," I whimper.

"Why not?" she says, not unkind.

"I just feel like someone will alert him, it sounds crazy,

like I'm paranoid, which I am, but he always seems to know, and even worse, to get away with it."

"The reason I came here, to Scottsdale, is to get the final piece I need," I say. "The man is here. The man my friend was seeing lives here. So does his wife."

"And?" Janice is trying to understand.

"And I think the key to Alec, to get him to confess, is the wife. She's involved somehow. I'm still figuring out how."

I hear a thud on the garage door. I put the phone down. Someone starts pounding on it. I feel relief that the only windows are at the top of the stall.

"I have to go," I say into the phone. "He's here."

I press the 'end' button.

CHAPTER TWENTY

ALEC

MY PHONE RINGS. NO CALLER ID. I ANSWER ON THE second ring.

"I'm behind her." It's George.

"Should I meet you?"

"No. Going to find out." I hear a click. I know what that means.

I wait, alternating between pacing the room and sitting on the edge of my hotel bed rubbing at my temples.

George calls back again and tells me to meet him in her parking lot. He hangs up.

It is abrupt, the way it should be. Calls too short to trace, words minced.

I head to the address and wait—no reason for Levin to suspect the Suburban I'm driving or look twice at me.

The garage door is closed, and I see no sign of her. Did we miss her already? I scratch my head, annoyed. This continual hit and miss is a frustrating game.

I exit my vehicle and nod at George who has pulled in to meet me in the parking lot. He waits, patiently.

If Levin knows about Eric, then I'm already in a noose, ready to hang. We both are. I can't let her leave me thinking I'm a monster who killed her best friend. If that's the case, she has to go. There is no recovery from information like that.

Anyway, I have to know. It's why I'm here.

One of the many reasons.

George gets out of his vehicle. He decides to check her garage stall and peer in the tiny window slats above.

To do this, since he's not quite tall enough, he grabs a ladder that's leaning up against the garage on the end. He doesn't care if anyone sees him. He's not the one taking her.

I grin as I watch him hoist it against the front of the garage and look in. He is fast, a quick scan around and then he puts the ladder back in its rightful place.

He gives me a thumbs-up and walks back over.

"She must be in a different garage stall. A Hyundai Sonata's in this one, not the Impala. But garages on both sides are empty."

I'm baffled as I thought I had the correct spot. A string of cuss words come out of my mouth, pacified that she must still be out.

George decides to keep watch and will alert me if she comes home during my tour of the property.

Ambling around her property, blending in and keeping the same Arizona Diamondbacks ball cap on with worn sneakers, I pretend I'm a jogger about to go for a run.

There are plenty of dog walkers and people wandering through the complex. I keep a low-profile and decide to sit on a bench near one of the entrances and watch.

You can learn a lot just by hunting your prey. So many people are reactionary instead of proactive. I learned a lot after Heidi. I reacted, and it almost got me caught.

To hone in on the kill, you have to know it inside and out, watch its movements, and bide your time.

I keep a watchful eye on the condo community and decide to do my due diligence. I walk around noting the abundance of green grass, foliage, and walking trails intertwined throughout the complex.

Some areas are more shaded than others, but I am thrilled to find that Levin's place backs up to a small expanse of green grass and nothing but weeds behind it.

Even though she is on the second floor, only a handful of stairs lead the way up. A small balcony is attached to the double doors off the master.

It is imperative that even though Levin is not home, I enter her life once again.

This time, through her apartment. It's best I see what my dear girl is up to.

I check my surroundings. I know how nosy neighbors can be, especially when you live within shared walls and a sense of community.

I watch an elderly woman walk her ten-pound poodle mix and roll my eyes. These days, everyone mixes a poodle and calls it a 'breed.' Levin had been adamant that we get a golden retriever or lab mixed with a poodle, making it a doodle of some sort.

What happened to just getting an old-fashioned collie?

I nixed the dog idea for the time being. I didn't want it to take away from what we needed to focus on—inheritance.

Plus, I didn't want her to get too attached to it. Children were one thing, they needed you for survival, but if Levin had a puppy, all the affection would go to that, and I would suffer.

I climb the stairs two at a time and notice a welcome mat on her doorstep with a fake potted plant next to it.

George has supplied me with a copy of the key since he's already stopped by earlier in the day to put his hard-earned life skills to work. He used to hotwire cars and break in fast food joints with his magic touch. That, combined with the right tools, makes him the perfect con man.

The key fits perfectly, and the handle turns.

A whiff of her perfume hits me. It is gut-wrenching how I feel like I have been transported back to our house, a smell that is second nature to me, the Chanel fragrance a welcome aroma to my nostrils.

Inside, the place looks clean but outdated. The furniture is mismatched—white wicker with light oak. There wasn't a lot to see—sparse furnishings and only a few watercolor paintings. There is no carpet, just hardwood floors, and tile in the kitchen and bathroom.

There's a flat-screen TV in the living room and an alcove separating the living room and dining room. It is a small space, complete with a dented metal desk and a watercolor painting. A large, oak bookshelf towers over one wall making it the focal point of the small area.

No wonder Levin picked this place, her head is always buried in a book.

We fight about it sometimes, her getting swept up in written words and neglecting her duties as my future wife.

The refrigerator's practically empty save for a case of bottled water and a protein shake.

I head back toward the only three doors in the place. One is a hall closet with a vacuum and various cleaning supplies.

With a thud, I slam the closet door shut and move on to the next one, slightly ajar.

It's the bathroom with one door connecting to the hallway and the other door opening into the bedroom, a Jack and Jill, they call it.

There's a bathtub with a bar of soap, razor, and shaving

cream along with some travel-size bottles of shampoo and conditioner.

A toothbrush, toothpaste, and floss rest on the sink. There is a makeup bag haphazardly scattered with various blushes, lipsticks, and eyeshadow colors. My eyes dart straight to the bottle of Chanel. I longingly hold it to my nose, the smell of Levin and all her secrets housed in this bottle.

I spray it and inhale the soothing fragrance.

I smile to myself as I see her ratty old robe hanging on the back of the door.

As much I as try to convince her to throw it out and have threatened to toss it, that robe hung around like the noose that would be around her neck soon.

It brings me a level of comfort, so I sniff it. It smells like her body soap and lotion—a perfumed mix of lilacs and Nivea.

I inspect her trash can. You can learn so much about a person by what they discard, what they're doing, and where they've been. It is almost empty save for tissue and a couple of Q-tips.

The master bedroom is large and decorated in Native American prints. An Indian woman with a clay pot and a baby on her hip is depicted in a painting above the bed. There's a rocking chair in the corner that had been taken over by a mishmash of clothing. Shoes are laying on the floor in all directions, most missing their match. Much like our current predicament.

The dresser only has a few items in it, same with the walk-in. She hadn't brought a lot with her. I shake my head in disgust. How could she leave a good thing?

I had taught Levin to make her bed, and that was the only thing that was in order. I sit down hard as a burst of anger shoots through me as I think why.

If she isn't sleeping in it, then, of course, it wouldn't need to be made. I tamp down my temper as the sudden urge to rip the sheets off the bed and throw her clothes off the balcony enters my mind. I rub my temples and count to ten backward and forward.

Disposing of her items would cause a scene. There would be questions and knocks on the door. Easier to get rid of a body, if you ask me.

On top of the dresser, I notice her jewelry box, one of the only heirlooms left by her mother. A gaudy ring from Europe is nestled in the red velvet. It is mother-of-pearl, and her birthstone—emerald—is entwined in the middle. The color matches her eyes, but the gold is cheap and losing its luster. Plus, I'm pretty sure it came from a guy she dated on her travels. I thought she had gotten rid of it since I had insisted it was hideous.

To avoid a fight, I thought she stopped wearing it. I had strongly suggested it did not match her wardrobe and looked like something you would find at an antique show. That had shut her up, and she had altogether stopped wearing it on her right hand.

The only other piece of jewelry in the box was the diamond necklace Eric had given her when she had graduated college. It had been such a prideful moment for her walking across the stage, grinning proudly as you could see in the tattered picture that was folded up next to the silver chain. I finger it delicately wanting nothing more than to rip the fine chain in half. Instead, I pocket it.

A pit forms in my stomach as I feel the pocket of my shorts. The engagement ring is always close to me waiting to be reunited with Levin. Meant for her left ring finger, it is a symbol of marriage. Commitment.

Next, I inspect the balcony and double French doors leading outside noting the distance to the ground. There's nothing on the balcony—no outdoor furniture or even a plant. As I suspect, it looks straight out onto the green space.

Lucky for me there're no streetlights that would flood the grass at night. It looks to be just an open expanse of green leading nowhere except to a sidewalk. It has been undeveloped as of the present.

There's nothing else I find in the apartment. I peek out the curtains and check to make sure no one is outside her apartment before I exit.

CHAPTER TWENTY-ONE

LEVIN

WHEN I HEARD THE THUD, I SWIFTLY ROLL UNDER THE Hyundai. It's a large enough sedan. I made sure to keep my purse underneath me and my body still.

There's nothing else in the garage save for the vehicle. The vehicle that no one should know is mine.

Thank God there's not a side door in the garage. A break-in would be expected.

I have to countdown not to go into full-on panic mode. I don't know how long Alec or his accomplice is there. I start at one hundred and work my way backward.

One hundred.

Ninety-nine.

Ninety-eight.

Ninety-seven.

Ninety-six.

There's a scratching noise as something is being dragged away. I assume it's the ladder.

I hold my breath. What next?

The thought of opening the garage door is overwhelming, I touch my hand over my chest and try to slow the pounding. There's nowhere for them to go but in.

Footsteps recede.

I could get in the vehicle and back out real fast. Alec doesn't know that I know, though. If it's him, and I automatically run in fear, that's a dead giveaway, and the prize is... ding, ding, ding.

Death.

Probably death by hanging. Or death by choking.

He also doesn't know my Impala is sitting at Enterprise, and this is my new ride.

There's a parking lot that has two entrances and two exits.

I decide to risk it.

Safety's my main concern, and I feel uneasy, biting my lip and thinking about where to go.

I pull out. A quick scan to my left shows the Cadillac is backed into a spot. I keep my head down and head in the opposite direction. I don't dare look to see if the man is watching me, my arm is up on the window like I'm leaning on it. My finger stays on the garage door button, and I press it immediately keeping my eyes targeted on the rearview mirror to make sure it closes.

The cowboy is leaning against his vehicle, arms crossed, scanning his surroundings, and I hold my breath as he gets smaller and smaller, his reflection a mere dot behind me in the low light as night creeps in.

My breath comes out in a loud huff. I consider my surroundings and where to go. The police? Approaching uniformed officers still won't ensure my safety at this point. Alec is a brilliant mastermind. He's gotten away with murder before, he'd have no problem requesting his attorney and then coming after me once he's released after questioning.

I keep my eyes trained on the road in front of me but also peer in my mirrors to make sure I'm not being followed.

The resort seems to be impervious, a safe haven for me. I know there are cots set up in the employee lounge. Amada told me to head there, and she would call Maddy and tell her how to reach me. I park in the lot and topple out of my car, the dread I feel insurmountable.

It's dark, and I'm bone tired. And scared. My footsteps sound heavy on the concrete path. The resort is huge, and though it is welcoming during the day, at night, the seclusion is overwhelming. Especially when you're scared for your life.

Lighted luminaries lead the way, but I hit a dark patch, and every tree seems like an arm reaching out to grab.

'*Get it together, Lev,*' I tell myself, a harsh warning reverberating in my head.

As I'm walking through the heavy foliage, palm trees and shrubs, I hear footsteps behind me and almost scream as a hand reaches out and grabs my shoulder. My initial reaction is to swing. I hear a thwack as my arm connects with tissue. Then a thud. Then a moan.

I whip around, eyes wide with shock, my heart threatening to leap out of my chest. All I can think about is the cowboy. Or Alec.

It's not Alec. It's not the silver-haired man.

It's Jake. Jake Hunter. Villa 19.

Shit.

He winces in pain.

"Oh my God, *Mr. Hunter,*" I exclaim, "you scared me." I clap a hand over my mouth. I'm ashamed. And embarrassed.

He's stopped in his tracks and waves his arm in the air like I should continue. I don't, and I can't.

"I'm so sorry, Jake," my apology spews out. "I thought... I thought you were someone else."

"Unless you have a stalker," Jake rubs his face, "I have no idea why that would be your first reaction."

I nod but don't say anything.

He looks me up and down. "What're you doing here?"

"Running," I say.

He looks confused. "Running at night?"

"No." I look down at the ground, "I was going to go sleep in the break room."

"Is something wrong? Did something happen to your home?" Jake breaks into leadership mode, his voice firm.

I shake my head. I'm quiet. I don't know what to say. How to say it. What to tell him. He's a client. Involving him in any of this could get me fired.

"Look," Jake says, "I know you don't know me, and this is probably strange, but I don't want you to sleep in the break room." There's worry etched into the lines on his face. "Clearly, you have a situation. You can stay in the front room of the villa. I promise I'll leave you alone. I know you have a killer right hook." He tries for a joke, and I laugh, but it's forced, considering the circumstances. I can't believe I hit him in the face. I'm flushed crimson. Thank God, it's dark. I don't know what to say. I don't want Amada or Olivia to get wind of this.

Jake reads my mind. "This is between us. I promise." He puts a hand on his chest. "I can be discreet." Jake reaches down and pulls the key card out of his pocket, his other hand near his eye where I smacked him.

"Do you want ice?" I feel terrible.

"Nah," Jake says, "I'll tell my staff I took up jiu-jitsu."

I look around still uncomfortable about this situation.

"I'll head in." Jake understands my dilemma. "You follow when you're ready. I'll get the pull-out bed ready."

I start to protest, but he gives me a stern glance. This

look must be why he is so successful. I instantly close my mouth.

I head to the employee lounge and grab some ice. I bring it back to the villa.

True to his word, Jake got the front room ready for me. The bed is pulled out of the couch, and the blanket and pillow are already laid neatly on top.

I hear a knock between the front room and his main room.

"Yes," I say. "Come in."

"Hey, I have to be up early for a meeting, so I'll probably leave by seven," the skin near Jake's eye is starting to bruise, the color of eggplant appearing. I cringe. "Just wanted to give you heads-up since I'll have to walk through here."

"Mr. Hunter," I start to say. The gold flecks in his eyes shine back at me. He is handsome. "I mean, Jake, here's some ice." I grab a towel and wrap some ice chips in it and hand it to him. A grimace is on his face as he presses the Egyptian cotton to his contusion.

"Thanks." He turns to head to his room. "Knock if you need me." He turns back around. "Don't forget to deadbolt the door."

I don't realize how exhausted I am until my head hits the five-hundred thread count bamboo sheets. The day's events have my head spinning, and sleep is impossible.

Being riled up, my nerves are shot. I turn the TV on, then off, never settling on a show. Never calming down as I hear the voice of Kramer on *Seinfeld* reruns, his crazy mane and insane melodrama usually a go-to when I can't sleep.

I snuggle underneath the covers, counting again, a trick that sometimes works. It does not.

No games on my phone to alleviate the tension.

There's a couple of guidebooks and magazines on Arizona

attractions. I thumb through them trying to peruse a couple of the articles.

Even though my nerves are jittery, I feel oddly comforted in Villa 19, Jake Hunter and his muscles a few feet away if I need him.

My body settles, and I start to feel groggy, a sense of relief washes over me. I slumber. It is not a fitful rest, but enough that I don't dream of Alec.

Unfortunately, tonight I dream of Heidi.

In the morning, I hear Jake moving around getting ready for the day. I keep my eyes closed, remembering how long it has been since I felt safe while I slept.

I don't have any clothes besides what I was wearing last night. It's a plus the resort encourages us to get ready in the employee lounge where we can grab a fresh outfit. They don't trust us to keep our uniforms as pressed as they would like.

Jake knocks before he enters the main room. I haven't sat up yet, and my hair is sticking up in all directions. I try and smooth it down.

Jake looks at me with concern. "Did you sleep okay?"

I nod staring at his face. That shiner's going to be the talk of the company today.

"I'm sorry," I say eyeing his injury.

"I know." Jake hands me two towels. Smart man, one for my hair, one for my body. "Do you need anything to wear?"

"Luckily, they provide the uniforms. Gran Vita doesn't have washers and dryers in our condo units, so it's best they don't trust us to wash and iron them. I'll just change in the employee room." I pull my purse off the side table and rummage through the contents for my phone. "Can I borrow a charger to take with me? My phone is almost dead." The low battery display flashes on my phone.

"Yep, no worries. Take this one." He unplugs one from the wall and hands it to me. "I have one in my briefcase."

"Anything I can do today?" I see I have a missed call from Amada. I'll return it when Jake heads out.

"Anger management?" Jake grins, his teeth perfectly even and white. "I left an extra toothbrush out for you. It's on the sink. The blue one."

"No fair, that's my job." I offer a benign chuckle. "You're going to put me out of business."

"On second thought, I have some dry cleaning and also, a gala coming up. You mind picking out my attire?" He raises an eyebrow. "Nothing too flamboyant. I don't like purple. Except for bruises."

"No problem." I'm intrigued. "Is there anything I should know about the event? Black tie?

I help with a charitable organization, domestic abuse."

Jake winks. "Your secret's safe with me." The thought of launching the pillow underneath my head enters my mind, but I resist. I've already caused enough trouble. The fear of losing my job, being followed, and my life sentence with Alec crosses my mind. I crease my brow in consternation. He notices the change in my demeanor and says, "Can I sit?" He glances at the overstuffed chair next to the bed. I nod.

"You don't have to tell me what's going on, but seriously, if you need to talk..." His voice is kind. "I think you have my cell, but if you need anything, I'm a butt dial away."

"Thank you." My smile is genuine. "And I'd be happy to dress you for the gala. Am I only shopping for you or do I need to consider matching attire with someone else?" I'm trying not to trip over my words as I say this. I'm curious if he has a girlfriend, but it's none of my business. It doesn't matter anyhow. No one else needs to be dragged into my soap opera.

"Nope. We don't need to match." Jake laments, "It's just a woman I've gone out with a couple of times. I'm not good at relationships."

"Ditto," I say. His eyes bore into mine for a moment. I hold his gaze. He taps his fingers on the chairs and then stands up and salutes me. "Have a good day, savage."

I bid him adieu, lock the deadbolt, and shower in the massive marble bathroom.

The sunken tub looks like heaven, but duty calls. I brush my teeth, ignoring the orange toothbrush and grabbing the blue one as instructed.

My old clothes will work until I get to the lounge. I pick up his room, fold the bed back into its spot, put the blanket and pillow back in the closet, grab the dry cleaning, and head out into the sunshine.

I start my day off with a fresh change of clothes and a new lease on life. Or at least, I tell myself I have a new lease on life.

Maybe that man yesterday was random. Nothing to do with Alec. Or me. Maybe it was just the maintenance man. There was a ladder situated there for a reason.

Granted, I'm on edge and paranoid. It doesn't sound convincing, but I try to tell myself it could have been a coincidence.

Being out from under Alec's thumb is a relief. Realization dawns on me at how miserable I had become playing house with him. He started pushing marriage and a future, and I started pushing away.

The gorgeous ring had been a test.

Alec wanted to change me, mold me, into a better version of myself, or so he said. That better version is debatable.

So, I have learned to listen and change myself for others,

knowing full well that love and happiness are not aligned with pretending.

I had dated someone in college who was my first serious boyfriend. He had been sweet, caring, and completely overwhelmed by my relationship with Eric. It had led to heated fights and sleepless nights. Then it came to a head when Eric and I moved in together our senior year of college.

"But why don't you want to live with me?" he had whined mercilessly. It never ended, and after a few months, I couldn't handle the resentment in his voice. I had once again picked my gay best friend over a committed relationship.

But Eric and I, for all our differences, had an agreement.

We both came first with the other. Until someone came along that we could see ourselves with, then the other would take a step back. That hadn't happened for either of us until Eric had found Mark.

I still remember Eric coming out to me.

Frazzled nerves and sweaty palms as he tried to hold my hands in his. We were still in high school—it was our senior year. Though Eric and I had taken each other's virginity, we still had an innocence about us. That moment of us giving ourselves away to the other had been the purest form of love. We hadn't known anyone else, hadn't had broken hearts or broken others, we still thought love existed like in fairy tales.

I was a little more skeptical given my childhood, but I tried to believe in the greater good—that someday someone might be worth letting my guard down.

Eric and I had only made love once.

After that, it was awkward for a moment, as the gravity of what we had done set in. Our history saved us. It had been beautiful and good, and like an itch, we had scratched it in the desire to know what sex felt like. I could tell Eric was horrified that I had bled on his soft cotton sheets. I was mortified that I was somehow dying or pregnant from this, but he assured me he had put on the condom correctly.

When he finally sat me down, confiding in me about his sexuality, I was relieved. Our relationship hadn't developed into romantic feelings. I was worried there was something wrong with me.

I had always known Eric was a little off. He was awkward around most girls other than me. He didn't flirt. When girls took an interest in him because he was one of the best-looking guys in our class, he seemed taken aback. The few dates he went on, he never took them out again. They were 'nice girls,' but nothing ever materialized.

"How do you know they wouldn't accept you?" But before the words were even out of my mouth, I knew the answer. Eric's brother was a fuck-up and was in and out of jail and rehab. He had started smoking dope and then had transitioned to harder drugs before becoming a dealer himself. His parents had weathered a storm with him and then to hear Eric was gay, well, they were religious to a fault.

I had heard the comments his father had made about gay people, and I knew his mother would disown him. They were always pushing Eric to get a girlfriend, and though they tolerated me, I could tell they wished I would step aside for him to find a girl.

"Yeah, but no one can know." He gave me a serious look. "I mean it, Levin." He never used my real name. "No one can know. Only you. I don't want it getting back to my parents or the kids at school."

I nodded my head slowly. A fellow high school acquaintance had been beaten up pretty severely when he came out as gay. There still wasn't a tolerance or understanding at our high school and especially in our small, conservative town.

"Your secret's safe with me." I moved closer to him and wrapped my arms around his shoulders. "I promise."

And with that, I made the only promise I have ever made in my life.

Until now.

I made a promise to Eric that I would put Alec behind bars. He and Heidi both deserved justice. I had to get proof. Mark and his wife lived here. She was the key to putting him behind bars.

A recording, something that I could take to the police.

No one had wanted to believe me in the past.

CHAPTER TWENTY-TWO

ALEC

I DRIVE BACK TO MY HOTEL. THE ROOM FEELS claustrophobic, the flowered wallpaper closing in on me. I struggle to breathe.

The bed is calling to me, the weariness apparent in my slow steps to the bed, like I'm dragging my body through the coals.

The ring in one pocket, the necklace in the other. Levin, the common link between the two of us. I lay on the ghastly comforter that smells of mildew, pull them both out, threading the silver chain through the diamond band.

I've never been good at competing with others. I consider myself untouchable, so I avoid the thought of being the second choice, the next best. The fact that Eric's still the center of her universe irritates me. How she can leave a precious gem and keep this cheap necklace gets under my skin. I scratch at my arm as if Eric's a scab I can pick away. He's not even here, and he still haunts me.

The need to know what Levin's up to and who she's with suffocates me. I push a pillow over my head and howl into it, careful not to create a disturbance. I despise feeling weak—survival of the fittest—the strongest.

Weak is an adjective I'd use to describe Eric—not me—scared of his daddy, fearful of his boyfriend leaving him.

He wouldn't let the money issue drop with me. He kept hounding me about it. I tried to reason with him. He might be the financial backer—or more precisely, his parents—but I was the one who knew the business inside and out. Though a few deals had gone awry, it was Eric who had fucked us when he fucked the married man.

The client's wife is well-connected. Her father had been a business associate of ours which is the only reason that he, too, became one. He had referred Mark to us. Mark had walked in, pinstriped suit, pink tie, and had been nothing short of courteous. But it was clear there were undertones that Eric had picked up on.

It wasn't long before those client meetings turned into long lunches and dinners. Eric was slipping on his responsibilities to the business. Other clients weren't handled effectively. Eric was unresponsive to some international clients in town who came to us for business. Red flags were starting to rise.

That's when I decided to follow him, or rather, have George take an interest in him. I suspected Eric was gay at times—he had dated plenty of women, but none had stuck. He also seemed apologetic when they left like there was a constant theme to their leaving. I couldn't put my finger on it. He didn't treat them bad, I just assumed he had a three-inch cock or was bad in bed.

His relationship with Levin concerned me at first. They talked and texted a lot. I thought maybe he pined for her, and she was the one he put on a pedestal. Maybe no one measured up, and everyone fell short.

He and Levin had an easy banter and a past, but their relationship mirrored more like brother and sister. They acted like family and at times, fought like family.

Eric was softer and sweeter when he talked about her. He got annoyed at the men she dated, frustrated with her lifestyle choices, and her desire to backpack Europe—he was concerned for her safety.

George came back to me with the news that not only was Eric gay, his preference for gay clubs and gay dating sites like *Grinder* a definite indication, but he also had an affair going on.

Eric was sleeping with our client. I had thought maybe there was a mistake. Maybe they met up to discuss more real estate ventures and didn't want to include me. I didn't jive as easily with people as Eric did, he could remember tidbits and banter better.

The pictures didn't lie, though.

Eric and Mark locked in a loving embrace, fighting like cats and dogs in a parking lot, a mixture of hurt and resentment on Eric's face as Mark stared at him, guilt on his face.

There were more substantial pictures.

Normally, I wouldn't care what Eric's sexual preference was. After all, he was a grown- ass man, but it started to cause waves when he ignored our business.

I had a conversation with him about it, and he promised he would do better, that he had some personal issues going on. I acted naively and asked him if there was anything I could do to help. I feigned concern when he told me it would work itself out.

"Health issues?" I pressed. "Are you feeling okay? Have you been getting your yearly physical?"

He laughed. "Yes, bro, I have been. I just have been dealing with some family stuff."

"Is it Levin?" I played dumb. "She seems like a firecracker. I hear you argue over *FaceTime*."

"I wish," he said. "No, she's still in Europe, won't come back to me yet."

"Is there anything I can do to help?" I reached into my desk drawer. "I'm here for you, even though you're a pain in my ass." I pulled out a cigar. "Here." I handed him one of the Cuban ones his father had given us when we had started out. "Let's puff to the good life and a phenomenal year."

He accepted graciously and changed the topic to one that was always of interest to me—money, fortune, and the pursuit of it. I let the matter at hand go.

Until I got a visitor a month later—in our office.

CHAPTER TWENTY-THREE

LEVIN

I CALL JANINE BACK AND LET HER KNOW I'M SAFE. SHE'S near hysterical but says she'll communicate to Liz that I'm trying to put Alec behind bars.

Unless he gets to me first.

Amada is at work today, and we call Maddy together from her phone.

On my break, I use Amada's phone to look up Mark Manassas, the married man who Eric fell in love with.

He has an office about five minutes from where I am staying.

Today's about as good a day as any. I call his office and speak to his assistant. He owns a construction leasing equipment business. It started with his father-in-law, and he branched out on his own according to a Phoenix newspaper article featuring him.

His assistant, Molly, says he is unavailable today, but she can arrange a meeting tomorrow.

The only question—what am I seeing him about?

I tell Molly that I work for a large manufacturing company, and we are interested in the potential to explore leasing construction equipment for our new location. The lie slips off my tongue easily.

Thanks, Dad, for instilling the value of lying about your half-empty bottles and the fact your speech is slurred, but you haven't touched a drink for days.

The day drags on, my mind wandering off to Alec and his whereabouts and then to Jake. I hope mum is the word, and there aren't any repercussions on me staying in his room.

I still have a sense of nervousness about heading back to my place.

Since I am being followed, the idea of sleeping there seems ridiculous.

Should I get a hotel room? Funds need to be saved. Cot in the lounge?

Jake's room?

There's something about Jake, that even with all the turmoil in my life, I still am drawn to him and his magnetic personality.

I head home after picking up some dinner to go.

My eyes keep casting their glances in the rearview mirror. No one is following me that I know of—no silver Cadillac, no salt-and-pepper-haired man.

I decide not to park in the garage this time in case someone comes looking and puts two and two together.

I find an empty parking spot and make my way to my condo walking in nervous anticipation, my steps hurried, and my hand on the pepper spray in my purse.

The door is locked. I check the handle to make sure.

However, when I open the door, a sense of dread overcomes me.

It's times like these I wish I knew how to use a gun. Alec never wanted me to learn. He said he would protect me.

Now, I know why.

I walk through the rooms, pepper spray in my hand, ready to aim and spray.

The bathroom, though it seems untouched, smells like my perfume.

Obnoxious. Overkill. It's been sprayed.

Nothing's out of place but the lingering smell of my Chanel.

Maybe I'm imagining it. It has been a few days since I have spent time here getting dressed and ready in this bathroom.

I shake my head. Staying here seems like a bad idea. I won't sleep. I don't feel safe.

I start to grab some of my items and throw them in a duffle bag when I hear a knock.

I freeze.

CHAPTER TWENTY-FOUR

Alec

I drive to Levin's to wait for her to come home from work. The thought of watching her at the resort is enticing, but I'm not ready to be spotted. Yet.

Plus, workplaces can create ugly scenes, and I didn't want to draw attention to us. That's exactly what happened when Mark Manassa's wife showed up at my office. She was flustered and upset—a bad combination. She didn't bother knocking on my office door, just flung her arms wildly and screamed Eric's name.

At first, I thought she must be a jilted lover from Eric's past, but alas, she was Mark's wife. Her wedding ring threw daggers of light on every surface in my office as she struggled to regain composure. She wasn't beautiful now, what with all the lip injections and plastic surgery, but I could see she'd been a real beauty in the past.

I felt like she had punched me in the stomach as she explained to me that Eric was sleeping with her husband. My mind had trouble comprehending that he was sleeping with not only a client but this woman's husband. Her father had been the reason we'd been so successful. He had bought and developed multiple lots from us and referred clients with multi-million-dollar needs.

If her father found out about Eric and Mark, we'd be run out of this city, his connections would dry up, and our business ruined. I couldn't let that happen. So I made a deal with her, a deal that saved our business. Eric, not so much.

I must've fallen asleep, because next thing I know, the sun has set, and the moon is shining through the front windshield casting a spotlight on the complex. I wake up when I hear the thud of another vehicle going over one of those obnoxious yellow speed bumps.

I glance at my watch. It's after 8:00 p.m.

Shit, what did I miss?

A black Mercedes sedan is the cause of the noise and drives around the corner.

I decide to get out pulling a cap over my head. Her condo is on the second floor, but there are plenty of benches I can sit on. People are still out walking their dogs and meandering through the complex.

A man walks around the corner just as I take a seat. He is dressed in a suit and tie. There is no denying his good looks. He has light brown hair and is tall—over six feet. He looks confused.

He stops near me. Close enough I can smell his aftershave and cologne.

"Hi." He pauses and waits for me to glance up from my phone.

"Hi." My tone is short.

"I'm looking for someone." He glances at his watch. "Do you by any chance know where #236 is? Been a while since I've been to a condo complex." His eyes are apologetic.

I have every idea where #236 is. It's where my fiancée is supposed to be situated.

So this is him. He's tall, I'll give him that. That's about all he's got going for him. Anyone can wear a custom suit and call it good. He seems like a pussy, his lips too feminine and his skin too perfect like he's got an IG filter on it. Probably lotions his hands and jerks off alone most of the time.

Arizona is an open-carry state, and at this moment, I wish I had a pistol.

"I'm just visiting my sister." I throw my arms in the air, chuckling. "Who can find anything in this maze, am I right?"

He nods, but he's already walking away. I watch him go up the stairs, then disappear from sight.

I pop my knuckles. My left ear starts ringing.

The anger rises as I start to stand and head in that direction.

But something in me snaps.

I can't.

My knees are weak and give way. I slam back down onto the hard, concrete bench.

A moment later, I notice him heading back down the stairs confirming she is not at home.

The relationship between them is unclear.

"Sir?" I stop him as he starts to pass me.

"I think I might know who you're looking for." I tap my palm to my forehead. "There's a girl named Levin. Think she lives where you were, I'm just not good with remembering condo numbers."

At the mention of her name, he nods his head, eyes light up, his expression a grin.

"My sis knows her from the pool here."

I continue, "Such a unique name."

The man agrees.

"Can I give her a message for ya if I see her?" I force a fake smile. "She should be back soon. Or, could you text her?"

"I don't have her number." The man reaches in his pocket. "Can you just give her this?"

This is too easy, I think to myself.

Bulls-eye.

His business card with all the necessary info—name and number.

"Perfect," I say. "Think she just went to the gym."

"Oh, if it's here..." his voice trails off, "... I can just stop by there."

"It's not." I stand up. "It's a drive."

Getting this man's business card should be a fairy tale. Except it isn't. It's a fucking nightmare.

Who's this man to Levin?

The anger starts to build, and I ball my hands into fists bending the card in my palm. His card says Jake Hunter, CEO, and a solar energy logo for a company named SolarBright.

Ahh, this explains it all. Put a fancy title behind his name and, of course, women fall over him. I bet it's a company of one.

I'm trying to follow the therapist's advice, the only good piece of advice she gave—inhaling and exhaling deeply.

It doesn't work.

I haven't found any communication between her and other guys in her phone or email. I thought for sure I'd find something—some sign she was cheating or some reason for her to just leave me sick. But there was nothing. She didn't send that many emails, most in her inbox were spam or sales and coupons.

He shouldn't be here. She certainly isn't installing solar energy in this fucking place. I pull on my ear, tilting my head, commanding the roaring noise to stop.

I wait for him to leave, his black Benz exiting the gate. Lifting my phone, I snap a picture of his license plate just in case.

My pulse isn't slowing, and I decide to use the gym and get myself a release while I wait.

And wait.

And wait.

I pace around the complex walking circles around the area keeping my head down. No sign of her. The condo remains dark—no lights convey that she's home.

Levin doesn't come home tonight.

I'm sick to my stomach, the bile rising in my throat.

The nervous energy and unknown whereabouts of the one and only woman I want is making me sick.

What if I can't get access to the money? I always have a Plan B, but in this instance, I'm out of options, maxed out on lines of credit.

The house. I can sell the house, except it's mortgaged to the hilt. I might have enough proceeds to start over. Maybe in a foreign country?

I scroll through my phone examining old pictures. How happy we looked. Mega-watt smiles on both of our faces.

"Fuck," I mutter to myself. I pull out my wallet scrutinizing my credit cards and considering the amounts on each. A photo booth picture of us is tucked inside the money holder. They're black and white photos, each of us making funny faces into the camera.

Our happiness irks me now that she's abandoned me.

I rip it up into a million pieces, the diminutive shreds symbolic of how I feel at this moment. They float to the ground like puzzle pieces that can never be fit together again. She made me feel alive, and now she's somewhere testing my patience.

When I slide the wallet back into my pocket, I feel a

smooth, rounded edge. My pocketknife. Involuntarily, I smirk.

There's nothing more I'm craving than holding her down and running the smooth metal over her skin, the cold blade making marks that're visible to the world.

I want to cut her up, rip her into pieces, scar her and show off her flaws, the same way she's marked me for life.

CHAPTER TWENTY-FIVE

LEVIN

I LOOK THROUGH THE PEEPHOLE.

It's Jake Hunter, Villa 19. Instantly, I kneel down crawling back into the kitchen, away from any wandering eyes.

As much as I want to open the door, I can't.

If it's a work problem, it can wait until tomorrow. It's probably about an order or something he needs from the store.

I have a one-track mind right now, and it's getting out of here tonight. And getting out safely.

He knocks one more time. It's too risky for me to look out the window, so I sit in the dark and wait. I hear a thud as his footsteps retreat back down the steps.

I grab some of my items, and since my phone isn't a smart one, I offer cash to a neighbor I pass on my way out to send an Uber for me. She looks at me strangely, but I explain I left my phone at work and was dropped off here.

eems like a good idea. If anyone
longs to another condo.
wing where I'm headed, but
nt name and not a hotel. I can

to go. I'll grab the car in the

lge Caravan arrives, and the
my next destination, a hotel a couple of
minutes away.

The top floor provides me views and though sleeping in Jake's room would have been welcome, if only for the safety aspect, this also works.

The persistent shaking in my arms subsides, and I start to calm down. The deadbolt is locked, and I know if anything, I need to catch up on some zzzzs. This murky feeling will cause me to let my guard down, make erroneous mistakes. I have to stay ahead of Alec.

I take a Xanax and fall asleep. The pepper spray is nestled beside me in bed, the curtains drawn.

Tomorrow I will have the evidence I need.

Alec will be arrested.

I can go home. Wherever that is.

In the morning, I wake feeling energized for the first time in a while. The cobwebs have cleared, and I feel a renewed sense of purpose.

Today I will meet Mark Manassas after work. I want to make good on my promise to the memories of Heidi and Eric and their families.

When I arrive at work, I have a message that Villa 19 needs my assistance.

I knock on Jake's door, and he answers promptly.

"Hey," he says holding a cup of coffee in his hand. "Come in."

I enter almost feeling like a stranger. I hate the fact I feel vulnerable, that I brought a perfect stranger who could ruin my position at the resort into this.

Sleeping with just a door separating us the night before last was intimate, yet it's a separation of more than just a door between us. I'm on the lam, and I will never forgive myself if something happens to Jake because of my affiliation with Alec.

No one else needs to get hurt at the hands of my ex-fiancé.

He points to the sofa. "Please sit." He heads to the coffee pot and turns to me. "You want some?"

"Sure." I hesitate.

I stare at the walls pretending the abstract painting requires my attention.

He seems awfully formal today. Is *he* upset about the other night? The fact I pretended not to be at home? He decided I shouldn't handle his service? I brought this all on myself. I sigh.

He tilts his head watching me.

I decide to move to a more neutral topic, though not the best reminder of one of our first interactions.

"How's your head?" I pull my gaze from the painting, a glance at his face confirms the swelling's gone down.

That's a plus at least.

"Good." He gives me a tight smile. "A couple more days, and it'll be gone."

I nod, trying to decide if a joke is welcome. I open my mouth and close it.

"I have a confession." Jake is contrite. "I went to your place last night. To check on you."

Playing dumb is useful in this case. I act floored.

"I wasn't there," I offer.

"I know. A man told me you were at the gym." He raises his eyebrows. "Did he give you my card?"

"Card, what card? And what man? A neighbor?"

"A man said you were friends with his sis."

The color drains from my face.

"He was sitting outside your place," he adds.

Fear in my eyes is now palpable to Jake. I start to shake. My words are unclear, and I stammer to get them out. "What man?"

"Oh my God, Levin, I'm *sorry.*" Jake runs his hands through his hair in frustration.

"What card did you give? Like a business card?" I can't see straight. The room starts to blur. I lean down, head in my hands, wanting nothing more than to curl up in a ball.

Jake instantly moves to my side and touches my arm.

"Levin, what's going on?" Jake asks. "Yeah, it was my business card. Just name and phone."

"He's going to find me," I whisper. "He's going to find *you*."

"Who?"

I don't answer.

"I want to help you, but you have to tell me what's going on." Jake reaches down for my chin and moves my head up gently. "We can figure this out. If someone's bothering you, you have to stop running."

"Yes," I breathe. "But that's the problem. He likes to chase."

"Then we have to catch him at his own game." Jake's voice is level. "Levin, you need to tell me *everything* so that I can help you. It's obvious you're in danger. *Talk* to me."

Jake rises and marches to the desk grabbing the receiver. He dials '0' and waits a second.

"Hi, this is Jake Hunter, Villa 19. My secretary called out

today. Is that okay if Levin assists me?" He listens and then puts the phone down.

While he is doing this, he starts texting on his cell.

"I'm canceling my morning appointment." He puts his hand over the receiver when he says this. "No one likes breakfast anyway."

He disappears for a minute and comes back. He has a glass of water and a blanket in hand. He wraps the blanket around my shoulders and hands me the drink. Even though the room isn't frigid, my body temperature says otherwise. I can't stop shaking.

Jake sits down on the footrest and moves it closer to me, eye level so he can stare at me as I speak. The gold flecks of his irises are burning like a lava lamp that has been shaken and is now amalgamated.

I hesitate, not wanting to bring him into this mess. Not wanting him to think I am crazy.

What does it matter? I'm feeling sorry for myself. I'm dead anyway. Dead girl walking.

I don't want him to get hurt.

My eyes lock with his. There's warmth and compassion. He waits—waits for me to begin.

I open my mouth, and I start. The words tumble out. All my angst and trepidation are unloading onto Jake.

The pupils of his eyes are augmented, and his mouth drops open when I tell him I'm on the short-list to be murdered.

CHAPTER TWENTY-SIX

ALEC

LEVIN COMES TO WORK BUT ISN'T IN HER IMPALA, IF THAT'S still what she's driving.

She exits from an orange Dodge Dart, her brown hair twisted up in a bun and wearing street clothes, jeans, and a tee.

Whose car is this?

I make out the Uber symbol.

Did she spend the night with that man?

I pull his business card out of my pocket, a crushing urge to rip it up and toss it out the window overcomes me.

On a whim, I block my number and dial Jake's number. The number goes straight to voicemail. Probably a good thing. I have no idea what I will say.

The resort is spread out with lots of walkways, and I head into the lobby, cap down, shades on, and grab a map from the concierge desk and start to acquaint myself with the resort.

Where did Levin go is the main question on my mind.

There are three pools—one lap, one adult, and one with waterslides. I pass a tennis court and grab a racket laying haphazardly in front of the fence.

Immersing myself into these surroundings is a must.

There's an employee entrance, and I scope that out. My diligence pays off, and a couple of minutes later when I am glancing at the events board for the resort, I see Levin exit the employee entrance.

She's now dressed in what I can only discern is her uniform. White tennis skirt, Lacoste polo, hair now in a rigid bun instead of a messy one, and Converse sneakers.

I move behind a palm tree, so she doesn't see me, examining my racket, head down, shades covering my face.

She's with a Hispanic woman who's easily pushing forty. They are walking and talking, but it's the trickling fountain beside me that drowns out their conversation.

I keep an eye out and watch where they head.

Levin stops in Villa 17. Then knocks on the door of Villa 18. She's in there for a few minutes. Then Villa 19. I wait impatiently, but she doesn't exit.

A maid pushes a cleaning cart past, one wheel wobbling. Still no sign of Levin.

My irritability grows. I start to sweat. It's still so damn hot.

But then a man exits Villa 19. The one from last night. Jake Hunter.

He's dressed in a suit again carrying a briefcase. He looks distraught. I watch him pull his cell phone out and punch in a number.

I hear him say, "Detective."

What the fuck.

Why's he on the phone with a cop?

My paranoia sets in. A coincidence, maybe? But this hits too close to home to be a coincidence.

Levin still hasn't exited the villa. Is there another way out?

Jake doesn't come back.

The maid service is making their way to Villa 19. They knock. No answer. They enter.

Glancing around to ensure no one's watching, I head in that direction.

This is my way in.

CHAPTER TWENTY-SEVEN

LEVIN

JAKE'S THE PERFECT LISTENER. HE DOESN'T INTERRUPT, except for clarification at certain points. He is stoic, and though his eyes widen, and he wrings his hands, he doesn't act histrionic. Exactly what I need.

Tears stream down my face at parts in my story, namely the gruesome discoveries of Heidi by her roommate and then Eric's violent death. My voice shakes, but I soldier on telling him only the highlights if you can call them that.

The blanket wrapped around me envelops me, and so does Jake's comforting stare. He doesn't make any sudden movements, but he takes my hands in his when I'm done speaking.

"Levin," Jake's soothing voice says, "I have a friend who works in the PD here. He's a detective. I'm going to call him. I know you want to get proof, but your life isn't worth it."

I nod my head, knowing he's right.

"I hate leaving you right now, but I have an afternoon

meeting with the board," Jake says. "I don't want you going back to your place. Stay here."

I begin to protest but stop. He's right. I'm safe in his villa. At least for now.

Jake squeezes my hands and stands up. "Call my cell if you need me. I'll be back in a few hours. If there's anything you need to pick up from your place, we can go tonight."

I give him a taut smile. He caresses my cheek and grabs his briefcase before he heads out, his footsteps hesitant, his body language unsure as he doesn't want to leave me here.

My body refuses to move from the couch, and I sit and cry for a couple of minutes, releasing the pent-up frustration and dread that's taken over my life.

He isn't gone long before there's a knock on the door. Through the peephole, I can see it's the maid service.

I'm in my uniform, and I quickly wipe my cheeks of their tears and start organizing Jake's clothing as they come in and clean.

It doesn't take them long as his place is barely lived in, the bedding the only sort of disarrangement in the place.

As I finish up the closet, Amada calls and asks if I can meet her in the employee lounge. I head out the French doors in the master bedroom as they go directly onto the path, and this keeps me out of the way of the cleaning crew.

The two women holler at me as they are leaving. The door clicks shut behind them. As I am shutting the French door behind me, I hear the door open again and a thud as someone enters, but I don't turn around. Maybe they forgot cleaning supplies in the room?

CHAPTER TWENTY-EIGHT

ALEC

I WAIT UNTIL THE MAIDS HEAD OUT. THERE'S TWO OF them, both speaking in Spanish. I assume Levin will follow behind them, but when she doesn't appear, I exhale racking my brain as to where she could've gone.

I am perplexed at this—is she in Jake's bed waiting for him to return? A conniption fit is threatening to erupt. I grab my left ear and twist it hard tugging it. The buzzing in my ear's starting, reminding me that I'm like a dam about to burst, the negative energy threatening to release a shit storm of emotions, all detrimental to my well-being.

And Levin's.

When Jake left, he was clearly dressed for the office. Solar energy, I think it was. What a scam.

As the maids exit, I pounce. I pretend like the room is mine and nod to them. I hand each a twenty-dollar bill and smile. They are appreciative, they giggle and say something in broken English. The cart they are pushing is full of extra items and towels. I shrug my shoulders to the door and motion that I don't have my key.

There's a pause as they glance at each other unsure if they should let me in.

I make the motion of a shower since I am sticky and sweaty and have the tennis racket in hand. I find another fifty in my wallet and hand it over. That does the trick. They use their card, and I enter Villa 19.

Wondering what good explanation there could be for Levin never coming out, my eyes drift over the front room. It is a big room, with an overstuffed armchair, matching footrest and couch that take up a majority of it. There's the requisite side lamps and a small kitchenette with a mini-bar.

I stride over to the desk. There is an invitation to a gala tomorrow night for a Mr. Jake Hunter and his plus one. Is my bride his plus one? I ball it up in my hand.

A lone key card is next to the phone. I snatch it up and put it in my pocket. This should come in handy, you little minx.

Besides the invite, I see nothing else of interest. A laptop bag is on the chair, but besides that, the place is empty.

I rummage through the laptop bag, but nothing but a charger and a few errant receipts are stuck in the front pocket.

I hear a squeak and then a clunk.

Someone is here.

I make my way into the other room. There is a light on in the master walk-in closet. Nothing but men's clothes hang in their apathetic dry-cleaning bags.

I realize I am carrying the racket in the other hand and set it down.

There is no one in the bathroom, no women's items are strewn on the counter. I notice two toothbrushes on the sink.

That's odd. Maybe one is for a travel bag and one is from the hotel?

I get on my knees and check under the bed, half expecting to see Levin's brunette hair peeking out from under the bed skirt. Nada.

That's when I notice the French doors leading out to the patio are slightly ajar. They are behind a billowy curtain, and the door is out of alignment.

I sit back on my heels.

So, she was here. And it's obvious she's on the lam from me.

This answers my questions.

You bad, bad, girl.

I bite my lip and throttle my hands imagining them wound tightly around her neck.

CHAPTER TWENTY-NINE

LEVIN

AFTER I CATCH UP WITH AMADA IN THE EMPLOYEE LOUNGE, I decide to go back to my place and get my car. I have to meet Mark later this afternoon, and as far as I know, the man who followed me is still expecting me to be in the Impala.

It's broad daylight, and there are lots of people out and about walking their dogs and strolling through the condo complex.

I decide to run inside and pack the few items I have, so Jake and I don't have to come here in the dark. I shudder involuntarily, thinking of Alec watching my every move.

When I get back to the resort, my thoughts are jumbled as I park the Hyundai and walk back to Jake's villa.

The sound of kids splashing in the pool is missing due to the time of the year. It's fairly quiet for October, though some guests are walking to the spa.

I use the key card that I was provided on my first day to enter Jake's villa. It's not as welcoming without Jake in it.

The shades are drawn, and the dark is inviting as I walk through the place, my thoughts tripping over each other. Why did Jake have to be so damn handsome? And kind? And a distraction from my nomadic life?

Though I'm feeling calmer, a distraction of reality television or a warm bath to wash away the muscle tension seems like the perfect idea. Lucky for me, I don't have to choose. There is a television hanging in the bathroom, it's placement right where I can see it from the bathtub.

It's a sunken jetted tub, and I plug the drain and turn on the faucet. Water pours out, and I busy myself taking off my uniform and setting my clothes in a neat pile. I consider locking the door but don't because Jake still isn't due for a few hours.

My body settles in the warm water, and my eyes flutter shut, the exhaustion of the last few weeks is apparent. They stay closed savoring a break from the light and the tears that threaten to start again.

The television is on, and though I hear the sound, it is background noise, a remedy for my churning thoughts.

I don't hear the click of the front door as it unlocks, the door handle turn, or the footsteps on the padded carpet.

There are ten seconds of heaven where I am tuned out. Ten seconds too many.

The door to the bathroom is flung open and slams against the wall hitting the foiled wallpaper.

When I open my eyes, I already know, but I don't want to. I pray it's Jake, and he's excited to share some good news.

It's not Jake standing over me. It's him.

CHAPTER THIRTY

Alec

She looks so forlorn in the tub, unmoving. I'd think she was dead if I didn't know better.

Her eyes are closed, hair up on top of her head, resting in a catatonic state.

They don't fly open even when the door does.

I half-expected Jake to be in the tub with her. I'm glad he's not as that just would complicate matters.

She opens them languidly like a cat lazily flicking their eyes after a nap. She doesn't open them at once, but slowly lifts her lids to meet my eyes. They flash with recognition and fear.

I ready myself for a scream that doesn't come. It's as if my presence has sucked all the air from her lungs.

We stare each other like a contest to see who can last the longest.

Enough.

She squeals as I reach down with gloved hands grasping her around the throat as she tries to fight me.

Her skin is wet and slippery—a bad combination for my leather gloves. She's not in the best position, so her blows don't do anything but anger me. I'm tempted to squeeze her neck until her veins pop and she goes limp, but that would defeat the purpose.

I haven't decided on her punishment yet.

She looks at me, dead on, as her irises lose their luster, and I relax my hold on her. When she finally stops thrashing in the water, I stuff the rag with chloroform in her face shoving it down her throat as she chokes, her body flailing in the water.

I know it will take a few minutes to kick in. In the meantime, we can watch these housewives and their drama. I hate to admit it, but I find the women on these reality shows to be entertaining and mean-spirited. They know how to stay relevant, and I admire them for that.

"Baby," my voice is tender. "You know you belong to me. What made you think you could *just* leave?" I wait for an answer and then laugh as I realize she can't respond.

She's passed out, and her body would have slid down in the tub if I didn't have her locked in my arms.

Levin still looks beautiful even dead to the world. Like a mannequin, freckles spread across her nose, pale skin luminescent, hair gathered on her head, tendrils falling out of her bun.

With her eyes and mouth closed, she resembles a delicate life-size doll. I can't wait to play with her. She seems so pliable now that she isn't fighting me. If she hadn't fought my love, this never would have happened.

Despite her perfect physique, she's heavier now that she's dead weight. I glance around trying to decide if I should bring anything with me. I take her purse and check for a cell phone, but the one I locate isn't her iPhone—it's a flip-phone straight out of the early 2000's. The car keys to a Hyundai Sonata are laying on the counter, the rental agency's keychain attached to them.

Hmm, so that's why I couldn't find you.

I'm worried someone will see me leave with her, so I decide on exiting out of the French doors. It is fairly secluded back there and leads to the parking lot. I don't want to run into a pesky patron, especially when she can't walk or talk. The door will automatically lock behind me so there would be no sign of forced entry.

To get her out of the tub, I have to pull her out being careful not to slam her head against the fiberglass side. I'm tempted to hold her under the water and drown her, but dollar signs keep me in check.

A silk bathrobe is hanging on the hook behind the door, so I put that on her body after I towel dry her off. I can't leave with her naked—at least the robe gives me something to grip.

She might as well be a sack of potatoes from the way I carry her propped over my shoulder. Carefully, I glance around before stepping out into the sunlight. Jake made the right decision to leave when he did. I wish I could've done this tonight with darkness as my witness, but opportunity doesn't knock every day.

The suburban is parked close by, and I put her in the cargo space, a blanket covering her.

And then I call George.

"I got her." If he could see me, he'd see the mile-wide grin claiming my face.

"What do you mean?" He turns down the noise in the background.

"She's in the back of the SUV."

"How is she?" George is alert now.

"Good. We had a nice, long talk, and I think we're on the same page now." I smile through the phone. It didn't matter that our conversation was wordless—one-sided—if you will.

"What's the next step?"

"This sounds crazy, but I think we're going to get married and put all this nonsense behind us. Seems like the logical next step, don't you think?" I don't wait for him to respond, his opinion unwarranted and unnecessary.

"Is that right?" George is floored at the turn of events but keeps his voice even.

"Yep." I buckle my seatbelt. "I'm taking her to the house I rented. How 'bout you round up a priest for us?"

George whistles. "Damn, that's fast. You still got the touch."

"And, George," I say, "I hope you'll do me the honor and be the witness and best man."

"Of course." George hangs up already moving on to the next task.

I admire the man and his willingness to be a team player.

There's a home in the mountains, not far from the resort Levin is working at, and that is the next stop. It is secluded and guarded, yet close to the city—a perfect combination of peaceful and remote.

On the drive there, I play some Mozart and try to relax, my fingers thumping the steering wheel.

Since there is a guard gate at the entrance to this particular group of homes, the road to the house is well lit. I don't want the security guard to ask any questions or see her body. I pull over on a deserted stretch of road and get out.

To be extra safe, I roll her into a ball. Her breathing is slow and labored. I tie her hands with rope just in the off chance she wakes up before we arrive at our final destination. Then I secure her feet.

I get back into the driver's seat and crank the radio. I am

done with Mozart and his symphony. I need uplifting. The rap music gives me a headache, and I can't stand today's country ballads about the good old days. There's an oldies station playing a song that's fitting for the moment.

"*You don't own me*" the singer wails as she sings about a controlling man in her life.

A smirk plays across my face. Everything is right in the world.

And Levin is mine again.

CHAPTER THIRTY-ONE

LEVIN

I WAKE UP IN A BED THAT ISN'T MINE.

At first, I'm hopeful that I'm in Jake's bed, that maybe I passed out in the tub, and he carried me here.

But then I remember Alec.

The realization that I'm somewhere unknown is crushing, and I involuntarily gasp.

My head throbs, and when I try to get up, I can't. I'm tied to a four-poster bed.

The room's darkness envelops me. Black is all I can see, liquid ink pouring out of every crevice.

Judging from the silky material resting against my skin, it would seem as though I'm wearing a robe and nothing else.

My mind races, replaying the last thing I remember—Alec standing over me in the tub. I attempt to scream, but my mouth is covered with tape.

I taste cotton and the remnants of something sweet.

Where the hell has he taken me?

I hear a squeaking sound, and a shape materializes as it comes closer to the bed. The mattress underneath me sags as he sits down.

"Hi," he jovially says as if I hadn't just discovered I'm bound and gagged. "I missed you *so* much, baby." He leans down to hug me, the glint of a knife in his waistband visible even in the dark.

My hands are tied above my head. I can't move.

I try again to scream. Nothing comes out.

"I want to take the tape off, but I don't think you'll behave." He tilts his head at me. "*If* you don't behave, off with your head." He makes a slicing motion across his neck and then laughs maniacally.

I close my eyes. How could I have been so stupid? He killed two people—that I know of. Why did I think *I* could get away from him? That he wouldn't kill me in a heartbeat?

He doesn't know what love is. He's crazy, and crazy people don't rationalize the same way others do.

When my eyes open, he is staring at me. In the dark, all I can see are the whites of his eyes. I wonder if I close them again, will he disappear?

"Let's play a game. If you blink once, that means yes. Two blinks mean no." A small bath of light appears as he turns on a bedside lamp. "Show me you understand," he demands.

I oblige and blink my eyes.

"Good girl." He grabs my leg roughly. "Now, can I take the tape off without you screaming?"

I blink my eyes once for yes.

"If you don't behave, I'll throw you off the side of the mountain, and your body will hit every rock on the way down. If you don't die from that, which I'm confident you will, a cougar or badger will eat your body. Do you understand?"

I believe him. I blink again.

He rips the tape off my mouth. I gasp, my skin feeling the sting.

I try to make out the room I am in. There is nothing familiar about it. It is large, and there are blackout curtains on the windows. Hence, the reason not a trickle of light escaped through the blinds.

Alec is dressed in black—black pants and a black long sleeve t-shirt. He is wearing combat boots, and a cap covers his hair.

The face that I thought was once handsome looks like a crazed joker to me.

"I missed you, did you miss me?" He commands my attention.

I blink once.

"You can stop blinking and talk, silly." He laughs and kisses my closed lips. I have the urge to bite him but resist.

"We need to talk, Levin." His tone is serious, but his eyes are maniacal. "There have been breaches of trust on both parts, but I want us to move forward with a renewed sense of purpose."

I can only nod. My gut is on fire, and I attempt to swallow, but my mouth still so dry. Killing my best friend and kidnapping me hardly sounds like a trust issue.

"If I help you sit up, will you be good?" he asks.

"Yes," I manage to spit out.

He pulls the knife from his waistband and cuts the rope on one wrist, helping me into a sitting position, but re-ties me to the post.

"My head hurts." My voice is hollow.

"Oh, baby, I didn't mean to hurt you." He coos at me like I am a small, helpless child.

"Do we need to be here?" I plead. "Can't we go home?"

"Home?" Alec replaces the knife in his waistband. "Do you miss it?"

"Yes." I lie. "It's the only home I've ever had."

"I didn't know you felt that way." He grabs my cheek roughly. "Couldn't tell since you *left* it and me."

"I left because I got scared." Now it was time to put on an Oscar-winning performance, lest I be murdered for not playing the right role. I shift my eyes downward. "I was worried I'd be a terrible mother and a disappointment to you."

"A terrible mom?" He stands up and starts pacing the room. The floors are hardwood, and his footsteps are heavy as they cross it.

"My mother, she wasn't the best," I add. He knows my life story, but a reminder couldn't hurt.

Alec pauses next to the bed. "It's not going to be like your childhood, Levin. We *aren't* your parents."

"Maybe it's selfish, but I could only picture being stuck in my mother's trailer, never having the chance to get out." I sigh loudly and dramatically.

Alec eats it up. Unless he's pretending as much as I am.

And in that case... I'm screwed.

CHAPTER THIRTY-TWO

ALEC

I KNOW LEVIN HAD A TUMULTUOUS CHILDHOOD. THE SCARS are still intact, yet buried, but in this case, rising to the surface.

My perception shifts as I consider her views.

"This is why you left?" I am incredulous. If this is the reason, and she has no idea about Eric, then it should be smooth sailing from here.

But, I'm skeptical. I want to believe her, I do.

She and I, we aren't so different. Both of us come from vastly different backgrounds, yet we hurt each other because of our past experiences. Trust keeps shattering, it crumbles, and at our core, we both don't have faith in each other.

I want to feel relieved, but I'm in shock. This is not the conversation I expected to have.

"I'm also worried I can't conceive." Levin looks ashamed, her head down.

"Why not?" I'm appalled. This is the first I'm hearing about this.

Levin takes a deep breath. "Jeff."

She only has to say his name once. I know all about him.

"Well, we can consult the top doctors." I sit down beside her. "There's nothing to be ashamed about. There's IVF if we need to. We have options."

Suddenly, I want out of the same room as her, the desire to punch a wall overcoming my sensibilities. I pull at my ear hearing the ringing shrill as it hisses at me.

The rational part of my mind tells me this isn't her fault. The irrational part of my brain screams that she's self-centered in not telling me her concerns earlier. This isn't the type of information you withhold from your partner, especially when we want children.

She starts to cry, inconsolable tears flooding down her cheeks. I caress her cheek.

"Please hold me." She tries to wiggle her wrists which are still bound to the bed. "I need you to hold me."

This was all I have yearned for since she left me.

Yet, at this moment, I'm conflicted. Is it worth marrying her? Should I just kill her?

If she couldn't give me children, then what's the point? Her spouse only inherits the money upon her death after a certain number of years.

The children were the golden ticket. They received the inheritance at birth. It was supposed to go into a trust, but I have a lawyer friend who could work some magic.

She senses my disapproval. "Alec? We can talk about this. We can talk about it all. I'm ready. I know I'm being selfish, and I'm sorry."

Her body looks so small and miserable tied up to the bed, the robe haphazardly open, exposing her breasts and a trail down to her V. Her face is splotchy from crying.

"I need some reassurance from you." I'm stoic even as she sobs.

She nods her head.

"I've given you *everything*." The spittle sprays her face as I start to heat up. "*Everything*, and you act like a spoiled brat."

She purses her lips and watches me.

I grab her cheeks, my fingers squeezing each side.

"You're going to start doing something for me." Her eyes don't leave my face.

"You're going to give me what I want."

I don't let go.

"Do you understand?" I move her face from side to side like she's a mere puppet.

Inside, I struggle with pulling her into my arms or strangling her for being such a selfish bitch. I'm just not ready to let go of her yet.

I slowly untie the rope that binds her arms, and I lay down beside her.

In her ear I whisper, "If you make any move to hurt or leave me, now, or ever, I will fucking kill you."

Her eyes widen, but she says nothing.

She lays her head on my chest, and I wrap my arms around her tightly. I have nothing to say at this moment. I'm spent.

The tiredness creeps in, and I am overcome with the need to sleep. I can't trust her to be on her own or watch me fall asleep.

"I'm going to get you some Advil for your head." I lie. I make a motion to lift her hands back over her head to restrain her again.

"Can't you just tie my arms together?" she whines. "It hurts to hold my arms up like this."

Before I know what I'm doing, I haul off and slap her

across the face. "Shut the fuck up. I'm tired of your whining and bitching."

She looks startled, a new side to my personality that had always been buried.

I typically didn't let my emotions get the best of me, at least in front of her.

My face softens, and I shake my head. "I'm sorry, baby. I just have a lot of emotions right now. Let me get you something for your headache."

I snap the lamp off dousing the room once again in obscurity.

I leave her tied up, eyes closed, as a bruise starts to form on her left cheekbone.

Fuck, the wedding pictures. Thank God for makeup. Levin would know how to camouflage it.

The bathroom in the master has a first-aid kit and a stash of different ointments and over-the-counter meds. I grab the bottle, so she thinks the pill is an Advil, but in reality, it's a strong sedative.

I bring the pills and a glass of water to her. There is wetness on her cheek, and I cringe. I hold her head up so she can drink from the glass, and she's greedy as she gulps it. I push the pills into her mouth.

"Swallow, baby," I say, closing her mouth around the pills. When I'm certain she's ingested them, I lay back down beside her. "We need to go to sleep and get our rest. We have a big day tomorrow. A lot of surprises."

I feel her body tighten up next to me. It's rigid, and I give her a peck on the cheek. I will let her stew this over in her mind as to what surprises are in store. But first, I want more.

My tongue flicks out of my mouth, and I search her lips. There's a pause, and I'm searching, seeking her approval. I need to know she wants me as much.

We kiss, and it's forceful, more so because I demand it. Her eyes are closed, and I'm sucking her face, drinking her in.

The pills will kick in shortly, and I shut my eyes, confident she will be out in a matter of minutes. They're horse tranquilizers. And strong ones at that.

CHAPTER THIRTY-THREE

LEVIN

I WAKE UP FROM A DEEP SLUMBER—MY BRAIN FOGGY AND my body numb.

Even though I'm certain it's day, the blackout curtains prevent the differentiation of light and dark from the outside.

My hands ache from their position, and though I tried to twist my body, Alec lies next to me, holding me down, even in sleep.

But he's is out cold.

My survival rests on me being able to play his game better than he can. I know that no matter what, I have followed his dark fantasies, fake emotion, insecurities, and love.

Haven't I done this my whole life? Pretend that I'm not dying inside? The practice I have in this area is not lost on me. I'm used to changing and adapting to situations that I have no desire to be in.

I can do this, I give myself an internal pep talk. I can add psychopaths to the list of people I have negotiated with. Alcoholics and abusers were only a starting point.

I decide my best bet is to snuggle into him, play the role of a repentant fiancée and try to convince him we need to go back home.

I wonder if he got ahold of my phone? What he knows?

My thoughts drift to Jake, and my stomach clenches. I wonder if he thinks I just went back to my place?

I clearly wasn't showing up for my shift today. Would Amada alert Olivia and Maddy?

Even if he doesn't kill me now, how am I going to pretend with this man—sleep beside him and feel safe?

These episodes will continue, me at his mercy. I wish now I had gone to the police. Trying to uncover even more proof had landed me in a maelstrom of regret.

Alec hears me rustling, and I watch his eyes pop open startled to see me awake.

"Good morning," I whisper in his ear. I figure starting out the day with neutrality is a decent route to take.

"Baby," I say, my voice a gentle murmur. "Do you mind if I pee? Also, I'm starved, so I'm betting you are, too. Anything here I can cook us for breakfast?"

He looks at me strangely. I'm hoping at the suggestion of food, I'm able to move off this bed. My arms ache, and my back is sore from the awkward way my body is positioned.

If he gets up and feeds me, I'll be able to move my hands, and maybe the numbness will subside.

He might even let me eat in the kitchen since he's opposed to eating in bed. I don't know if this rule applies in a kidnapping situation, but I sure hope so.

"You want to cook? You never want to cook." Alec shows his annoyance by giving my shoulder a rough shove.

"Alec..." I try my best for a look of remorse. "I fucked up.

Bad. I didn't let you in. I didn't do my wifely duties. Leaving made me realize how much you do for me, for us."

He nods his head in agreement. "You've been very bad. I agree it's time to start remedying the situation. You can start by apologizing to my cock." He motions downward and unzips his pants.

I start to protest but realize disobeying isn't going to win me any favors or buy me more time.

The disgust on my face is replaced by him shoving his cock into my mouth. He tries to find a comfortable position that keeps me tied up but able to get the job done.

The panic starts to rise, the feel of him in my mouth makes me gag. I'm imagining myself anywhere but here—Jake's face front and center in my mind.

I go back to my childhood—Jeff. The parallels between that universe and this not much different—I'm stuck in a situation that I have to fight my way out of.

A single tear runs down my cheek tickling my skin.

"Baby, I want to show you how sorry I am," I beg, "*Please* let me use my hands, too."

He pauses to think about this and reaches the same conclusion I did. Silently, he unties my hands, and I rub my wrists as soon as the rope is off. Jagged red marks throb across my wrists, and I wince.

"Baby, I'll take your pain away." He grabs my hair and pushes me down hard on his cock. I start gagging, and it excites him even more.

I pretend I'm somewhere else, anywhere else. I go back to my night with Jake. Even just being in his presence reassured me—yesterday morning—the way his hands enclosed mine, how he listened, his attentiveness.

He's the thought that's going to get me through this.

I shake as Alec's cum fills my mouth. I'm disgusted, but I

have a renewed sense of purpose. I'm going to get the hell out of here.

Alive.

CHAPTER THIRTY-FOUR

ALEC

AFTER I COME IN HER MOUTH, I WATCH HER FACE attentively. I know she hates the taste, so I purposely make her swallow.

She needs to be punished for running from me, for causing me pain, the lengths I've had to go to get her back, not to mention the money I've spent.

I drag her to the bathroom by her hair afterward, half of it spilling out of her unkempt bun.

She is grateful to pee, but she makes me nervous as she eyeballs the bathroom.

I eye her closely as she sits on the toilet, her face still red from my loss of anger the night before. She hates peeing in front of other people, it makes her anxious. I try to start a conversation to rush her along.

"You can cook me breakfast." I'm nonchalant. "Then we need to shower. Busy day today." She turns her face to look at me.

Her eyes search me for clues, for answers. She isn't getting an answer yet.

After she's finished in the bathroom, I bring out a pair of handcuffs and show them to her. "The kitchen is stocked. I want some eggs, over easy, and some toast. If you make any attempt to run, I'll handcuff you to the stove."

She nods, understanding.

"Get to work." I'm gruff.

I sit on a bar stool at the kitchen island and watch her. It takes her a minute to locate what she needs—the frying pan, spatula, and all the ingredients.

Before long, she's at the stove cracking eggs and preparing our meal. She does this with trepidation, tiptoeing around the kitchen in her bare feet, her silky robe coming lose as she keeps adjusting it to cover her body.

"Take it off," I order. "I'm tired of looking at it." She removes it without incident, and I throw it over the stool next to me.

She stands by the stove for heat, her naked body shivering.

I scrutinize her every move making sure she's not messing with the food or trying to harm me. All the sharp kitchen utensils have been removed for safety.

"Butter for your toast?" she asks.

I nod watching her bend over to get the butter out of the fridge.

"How should I spread it?" She's on the hunt for utensils. I'd already thought of taking ones that had the potential to hurt me out of the kitchen.

"Just like your legs," I joke. She shoots me a dirty look but wipes it away as soon as she realizes it. "Joking," I say.

She is confused as she looks for the knives.

"No knives," I say. "I'll use a fork."

She sits down beside me, and we eat in silence. The only sound is the clink of our silverware.

Her appetite shows, and she is famished. She even licks her fingers when she's done.

When I'm finished, I hand her my plate. "You can do the dishes."

She gets up without complaint. I'm starting to enjoy this exchange—me telling her what to do and her complying. Why hadn't I tied her up and demanded her loyalty six months ago?

There is silence minus the running water as she rinses the dishes. She's flustered as she drops a glass on the floor. It is plastic and bounces.

I give her an amused glance. This is a new look for her. I kind of like it, this uncertainty.

I've got the power. She's helpless, and it's sexy and irritating at the same time. The control I have, the way I can dominate her, turns me on and instantly, my cock hardens.

It's frustrating because there's not a shred of the hard-headed, stubborn Levin.

She has to bend down to get it, and I see her dilemma on her face. She is naked, and her ass will be sticking straight up in the air. Once that was natural.

I let out a frustrated sigh.

My tone's annoyed. "Pick it up."

She leans over, timid, and struggles to grasp it with her soapy hands.

As she straightens up, I come up behind and grab her ass. She jumps as I squeeze it.

"We need to get in the shower. Big day for us." At the mention of this, her eyebrows shoot up as she turns to examine me. She's confused and scared. This is the reaction I want.

The bewildered look gives way to one of complacency.

"Are you going to keep me in suspense or tell me?" Her nails are drumming on the kitchen island fidgeting impatiently.

I ponder the question for a moment.

Maybe I could tell her my idea. If she didn't like it, then we had bigger issues. Better to deal with disappointment sooner rather than later, I suppose.

Nah. I'll let her sweat the details for a bit.

She searches my face disappointed when I don't offer more. I put a handcuff on one hand and yank her behind me to the bathroom.

Because I need time to get everything ready, I motion for her to stand next to the towel rack. I snap the cuffs on the long metal bar.

"I'll be back soon." I see her panic-stricken face as she wonders where I'm headed.

"Baby," I gently stroke her face and hair. "We have company coming later. I have to be ready." Her eyes perk up at the thought of company. She is *dying* to know more. She might be dying later if she doesn't get in line, I think.

That's the problem—she's always hunting and searching for evidence unable to relax. I could tell by the cameras around the house that she's looking for something. There's stilted movements, long pauses, a scrunched look on her face like she forgot what she was looking for.

It's gotten her into trouble.

This time, it might not be a situation she can talk her way out of.

The reality is, Levin has all the power right now. She's the beneficiary. She decides—live or die.

CHAPTER THIRTY-FIVE

LEVIN

AFTER ALEC LEAVES ME CHAINED TO THE TOWEL RACK, I have nothing to do but wait. And overanalyze.

My wrists are already sore from the restraints. I twist and turn trying to get comfortable. The metal bar is cold on my back as I try to bend down and sit, my body hunched over, unable to do anything but shiver. Goosebumps cover my body, and I shudder.

Though I feel overwhelmed, it might not be the worst idea to have some alone time.

I need to formulate a plan of action ASAP.

Is there a landline in the house? Alec must have his cell here.

If so, I can call for help. Though I had only been in a bedroom, bathroom, and the kitchen, I was able to see out the small kitchen window. From my view washing dishes, I could see the house was built into the side of a mountain.

I had no recollection of the drive here, but it couldn't

have been too far. We certainly were not out of Phoenix judging by the mountains. This gave me hope. Maybe I can escape him.

My mind wanders as I think of what the surprise is.

And the guest he mentioned. Was it a former partner? Someone else he wanted dead?

Or worse yet, what if the gray-haired man showed up? That could be his hitman?

It didn't make sense, though. He had no problem getting Heidi and Eric's blood on his hands when he killed them.

Heidi, he strangled with his bare hands, yet he was never charged because he had an alibi—his mom. I'd ask her about that if I could, but she's dead.

Did she know and notice quirks as he was growing up that raised suspicions? Or did she coddle him making him think he was the center of attention, that no one mattered but him?

I'd always been curious about his parents' car accident. He seemed lackadaisical when I asked. I couldn't tell if it was because he buried the hurt or if he isn't affected because there's more to the story.

Yes, he staged the hanging to make it look like Eric had tied the noose around his neck and hung himself in his closet. That was a game prevalent in the gay world—asphyxiating yourself for a sexual high.

I survey the bathroom. This house has no expense spared from what I've seen. The kitchen is equipped with Viking appliances, high-end cabinets, and marble countertops. And the bathroom is no exception—the shower alone can hold a small army with its multitude of showerheads and long built-in bench.

The tub is deep and also meant to hold more than one person. Everything is marble and expensive-looking, the colors a soothing blue-gray. For some, this would be the perfect house.

I shake my arms and try and pull the towel rack out of the wall. Bolts hold it firmly into place. My hope that these handcuffs are the cheap play ones used to play cops and robbers as a child are dashed. They're not.

To my dismay, I realize they probably came from the police or industrial warehouse. There is no getting them off my wrist as evidenced by the bright pink flush creeping across my wrists. They cut into my skin which is already sensitive from the rope marks.

I use my feet as leverage to try to move the rack, and it doesn't even wriggle.

There is nothing to do but bide my time.

I'm stuck.

CHAPTER THIRTY-SIX

ALEC

AFTER I LEAVE LEVIN CONFINED TO THE BATHROOM, I RUSH to get everything ready for our ceremony. George has secured a priest and would bring him at 2:00 p.m. I alerted the guard so he would know and there would be fewer distractions.

Her dress is hanging up in another bedroom, and I walk into the room to inspect it. I tried to think of everything but am visibly overwrought by the idea of forgetting an item or trinket.

There's a bathroom inside this bedroom. I put my hands on the sink and look in the mirror. My face is red, and I'm crumbling under the constant pressure. A permanent scowl resides in the glass.

I take a breath and count to ten. The vows are what matters—that piece of paper that to some people is unimportant, merely a formality.

It's not in our case.

The promises we make today, in front of the priest, they seal the deal.

They're all I care about—my financial freedom.

I can feel the stress subside, the tension in my neck eases, and the constant drone in my ears subsides.

How do I communicate to Levin that she will be in a coffin if she doesn't fall in line?

The items are on the bed—a matching veil, garter, panties, strapless bra, jewel-encrusted heels, and a notepad so she can write her vows.

They need to be heartfelt and sincere—unlike this hiccup. It's appropriate for us to share some sentiments with each other, especially with all we've been through.

A quick walk through the house is necessary. There is only one way in—the massive, iron, double doors in the front. I check that they are locked.

I examine the backyard. It's pristine—backing up to the mountains, an oasis for one family to enjoy. A patch of grass is near the infinity pool, where we will exchange our vows. A perfect backdrop for a perfect day.

The excitement starts to creep in. We're about to be married—husband and wife. I smirk as I head back in to get Levin ready for her big day.

She's in an awkward position with her back against the wall, not quite sitting or standing. I chuckle to myself as I realize it's probably not the smartest idea to leave her to her own devices. What's the saying? Idle hands being the devil's playground?

"Levin." I tap her on the shoulder. "I want to discuss with you the plans for the day. Are you ready to hear them?"

She nods. She's naked and judging by the shaking of her body, she's chilled. I rub her back as I speak.

"To build our trust back, we need a solid foundation." I push her hair back from her face, the tangled pieces hanging down from her crooked updo. "Levin, this can only be accomplished by one thing." My jaw tenses as I speak. "We're getting married today. Time to be man and wife."

She's in shock. She just stares at me, her eyes wide. "Where are we getting married?" Her voice is barely audible.

"Here. A priest is coming."

"But I don't have a dress."

"I took care of it. I took care of everything." I grab the key out of my pocket and start to unlock the handcuffs. She slides down the wall with a loud sigh until she's in a seated position, arms curled around her legs. I join her on the marble tile, putting a hand on her knee.

She considers this and slowly, a grin creeps across her face. "We've *always* wanted to get married. Now we can just do it and not worry about all the planning."

She scoots closer to me. "Did you remember my ring?"

"I did." I grin. I like where her head is at. I thought I would have to warm her up to the idea. I didn't want her to be black and blue for the wedding pictures, but I would do what I had to do.

"Can we start trying, you know, tonight?"

My heart melts when she says this. I had planned on doing that, regardless if she was into the idea or not. Forcibly taking my wife isn't beneath me, especially when she belongs to me and my business longevity is at stake.

I'm enthusiastic, my face beaming. She's going to give me an heir. I cross my fingers for a boy.

"Of course, doll." I touch her leg and caress it. She doesn't shy away from my touch.

"Let's take a shower and get ready." Her wrists are red, both from the burn marks from the rope and the cold metal. I grab them and glance at her.

"I'm sorry about the accident last night." I lie. "Hopefully you can mask it."

She smiles, but it's forced. It doesn't reach her face.

I hold tight to her guiding her by the neck as we enter the shower. She immediately sits down on the bench as I hand her a razor to shave and shampoo and conditioner to wash her hair. I busy myself with lathering my body and start humming a tune trying to force the noise in my ears to die down.

"What should our wedding song be?" I pause mid-thought. She's soaping her body, and she stops as she thinks about it.

She gives me a peck on the cheek. "I know you know the perfect song, you organized this entire thing. It's only fair you pick."

"You're right, I've got it." I'm animated as I speak. '*Undying Love*' by Eddie Cochran. It was an old song, but the lines about eternity and unrequited love were fitting. I start singing the words to her.

She tilts her head to listen massaging her temples. She's quiet for a moment and then gives me a tight smile. "I think it's perfect. It fits us to a T."

I help her wash her hair, her arms fatigued from the length of time she was in bondage.

It's finally happening.

CHAPTER THIRTY-SEVEN

LEVIN

WHEN HE PROPOSED MARRIAGE TO ME THE FIRST TIME, I was shocked—thrown off guard.

When he proposed marriage to me this time, I was stunned.

Though there's the requisite part about 'until death do us part,' that might be sooner rather than later in my case.

I take my time shaving as my arms are sore. My hand shakes as I try to guide the razor over my stubble. This is the last task I want to do at this moment.

My eyes feel heavy, the lids burning. I'm unsure if it's the need to cry or what he used to wipe me out last night—chloroform—I assume.

He waits for me to finish, albeit impatiently. He's on cloud nine whistling and singing. He grabs a plush towel off the rack and starts drying me, furiously rubbing me with the soft material. He hands me some lotion, and I rub it on my body as he casts his eyes over me—head to toe.

"Is there someone coming to do my hair and makeup?" I try to sound excited like this is going to be the best day of my life.

He searches my face to see if I'm genuine, decides I am, and offers, "There's a bathroom off the room where your dress and wedding items are. You can get ready in there."

"May I have my purse, please?" I rush to get the words out. "My favorite lipstick is in there."

"I'll go get it. You stay put." He walks off closing the bathroom door behind me, still whistling.

This is my shot. I have to escape.

I don't know the layout of the house, but I know where the front door is. I had to pass it to get to the kitchen earlier.

If I upset him now, he will probably kill me.

But it's worth the risk. I'm a caged bird.

I make a run for it.

CHAPTER THIRTY-EIGHT

ALEC

I GO INTO THE STUDY AND FIND LEVIN'S PURSE. I UNZIP IT, and the Burberry checked plaid is barely visible underneath the plethora of items she's acquired. I could never understand why women needed to carry their entire wardrobe in their purse. It must weigh fifteen pounds.

I see a flash of brunette hair outside the door to the study, and I drop the purse and run. The contents spill out, and I trip over her makeup bag, smashing a compact mirror in the process.

Fuck, Levin's making a run for it.

She's erratic, her eyes delirious. She looks like a crazed lunatic trying to escape from a mental institution.

I'll let her hopes rise for a moment.

This place is like a prison on lockdown.

I shake my head. *Levin, Levin, Levin. You should know better.*

I'm ruthless in business, revengeful in love. I'd never let her parade out of here, at least not living.

The Taser I seized is in another room.

She is at the door fumbling with the lock.

How can she be so stupid as to think the door won't be padlocked?

Obviously, she doesn't think highly of me.

I'm hurt, the ire rising as I think of her pretending to want me. My entire life, everyone's been fake, concealing how they feel about me.

Counterfeits. I grip the door frame, the room spinning, a tune echoing in my ear on repeat. It's our wedding story.

I imagine Heidi's face. Then Eric's. They illuminate in front of me, their final expressions a reminder of their fate.

I reach out and spin her around slapping the shit out of her. She claws at my face, scratching me.

"You fucking bitch." I'm irate as I snicker. "You're dead."

"No," she's kicking out her feet as I'm grabbing onto her. She's hysterical, and it's incoherent, the words coming out of her mouth. All I know is that I'm seeing red, my blood on fire.

I punch her in the face, my fist connects with her jaw and knocks her out. She goes limp and falls to the floor. I don't want her to smash her body on the marble tile, so I catch her before she goes down.

She's bleeding, her lip is a bloody mess.

Her dead weight is a struggle to hold, so I pick her up and carry her into the bedroom with all the wedding items. I lay her down on the comforter sliding the items over to the other side of the bed. I place a towel under her face not wanting her to bloody the damask comforter.

The only person to blame is her. She's ruined our special day.

I leave the room to get a rag, soak it in chloroform and shove it down her throat again. She is breathing, but it's shallow and ragged.

With that, I turn and exit the room, locking the door behind me.

CHAPTER THIRTY-NINE

LEVIN

WHEN I COME TO, I AM ONCE AGAIN TIED TO A BED, THIS time, a queen size instead of a king in a different room.

The room isn't pitch black, but the furnishings are ornate and hideous like my fiancé. The bedspread has gold tassels, rose-colored flowers spraying across the heavy, draped fabric, and looks like it belonged to Queen Anne, the beheaded one.

I'm no longer naked. There's fabric covering my skin instead of a robe, I'm shrouded in none other than a wedding dress.

A wedding dress.

There's a gasp and a bloodcurdling scream as I realize I'm about to be the bride of Chucky.

No words come out as tape binds my mouth.

I am terror-stricken, my breathing shallow, and hives start to form on my skin.

I'm overcome with a feeling of claustrophobia—my body starts to hyperventilate. I can't breathe, and I'm choking trying to cough and having nowhere to expel my breath as I try to get ahold of my emotions.

The dress is ivory, a beaded bodice with a low-cut décolletage, short sleeves that are also heavily beaded. It's from a bridal magazine I bought a few months ago.

And it fits like it was made for me.

The gravity of the situation causes me to kick my feet out and pound the edge of the bed. I can't scream, and the fear is written all over my body convulsing like I'm having a seizure.

This sick psycho has been planning this for months. Regardless of me leaving him, he took care of our wedding without consulting me. He knew he was going to coerce me into marriage, one way or another.

I search the space for a sign of escape. This room has floor-to-ceiling windows, but I don't spot a latch—for good reason. If they did open, you'd fall to your death—good planning on his part. I could either fall to my death or get married. I was starting to question which one would be less painful.

The windows were all on the side facing down the mountain.

The clock on the nightstand shows it was a little after noontime.

I manage to pound on the wall behind me slamming my wrists into the drywall, banging my weak arms as hard as I can, knowing full well the repercussion is Alec storming in here.

There's a priest coming. Maybe he can help?

I notice the notepad and pen sitting on the bed nestled beside the undergarments. Maybe I could write the priest a warning?

I'd be reciting my vows. They should be private. What if I wrote a message halfway down, so it looked like it was all bullshit promises to love and honor my psychotic husband?

Would Alec ask to see them beforehand? My gut told me yes, he had already thought of this, always one step ahead of me.

Tears burn my eyes.

I freeze as I hear the door creak open, and Alec reappears, his face a mask of scratches and anger.

CHAPTER FORTY

Alec

Her face is frozen, dread etched on it by the taut look, tape covering any words she wants to let loose.

I stride over to her, ethereal in her dress, the unhappiest bride I've ever seen.

Fortunately for Levin, I've managed to calm myself down.

My demeanor is controlled, the earlier loss of control only present on her face, a swollen mass of blood and bruising.

"Stop." I am calm, my hands steady as I touch her hair petting her like a favorite pet. "You look beautiful."

My hands finger the delicate lace of her gown as I sit down beside her, the beading is exquisite. It was worth every penny. Just like her.

She twists to get away from me, her face haggard.

I rip the tape off of her mouth, and a gasp escapes her lips.

"We don't have long to finish getting ready." I ignore her

grunts. My hand folds around hers, and I say, "It's either marriage, or I can slash your face with my knife."

"If I marry you," her breathing's heavy, "then you'll kill me after anyway."

"No." I'm disappointed. I wipe a hand over my face. "Contrary to what you think, I love you. I'll let you live, though you'll be under watch."

"I don't want to live like this," Levin's voice cracks, her lips quivering, "... living under constant pressure, the stress of being under lock and key."

"You decide what kind of prison." I'm resigned. "But being married to me isn't a prison, Levin, at least, it wasn't before."

"Constant surveillance," Levin intones, "is still a prison."

"You had a good life." I'm detached, my voice sounds like it's coming from another person—monotone and level. "Stop acting like you haven't had *everything* you could want handed to you."

I start to hum a song ignoring her for a moment, not wanting to think about how our lives will play out, tied together in marriage or bound together by her untimely death.

My choice for the moment is to untie her. "I'm going to let you get ready. Hope you have enough concealer to make yourself presentable." She winces as I touch the bruise. Her lip is swollen, and the blood has dried. "I'll be back in an hour to get you."

The blade of the knife gleams as I show it to her, a gentle reminder of any missteps on her part. I hold my arms up scared she'll start pummeling me. I issue a warning. "If you pull any more stunts, you might as well have a death wish." I stand up. "Oh, don't forget to write your vows. Except death do us part. That goes without saying."

CHAPTER FORTY-ONE

LEVIN

THE LOCK CLICKS.

He's back.

I warily touch my hand to my face feeling the stickiness of blood. I am in pain—throbbing in my jaw, my wrists raw, and my chest is broken out in hives.

I search the room for an exit strategy and find none.

I'm stuck. My body is ice-cold like I've already died from drowning in sub-zero temperatures.

My hands shake as I hook my finger in the front of the gown.

The power of suggestion comes to mind. Something I read about imagining how you want a situation to go, repeating it, and willing it to be true.

I'm willing Alec to disappear along with this wedding dress. The thought of it crumpled in a heap, and my naked body soaring above Alec, my unhinged fiancé, is at the front of my mind.

In the bathroom, I slide down near the side of the tub burying my head in my hands.

A makeup bag is already on the counter filled to the brim with products.

I wonder if Alec found my phone when he took me.

He probably destroyed it.

I'm lost in thought, sure a witness has to be present at our wedding.

Ideas on how to get help come to mind. They all seem implausible. Alec will never let me out of his sight.

Except for this short amount of time before the priest comes.

The knock on the door startles me.

He sticks his head in the room as soon as I answer it.

"Don't forget your vows." He points a finger to the bed. "There's a pen and paper. Forget about asking the priest to help." He gives a maniacal laugh.

I roll my eyes. "Don't be ridiculous."

"I'll let you finish getting ready. You have a half hour."

With that, he pulls his head back out, and I listen as the lock clicks, and footsteps move away from the door.

My heart sinks. I want to throw myself on the bed, rip the wedding dress into shreds, and scream, yet all I can do is finish styling my hair and attempt to cover the contusions on my face.

I've never felt so alone in my life, the overwhelming fear of the unknown makes a cry escape from my lips.

Marriage to Alec—a death sentence—no matter what.

My throat hurts with a choking sensation. Even though no hands are wrapped around it, his invisible hands are already cutting off support.

CHAPTER FORTY-TWO

ALEC

I GIVE LEVIN UNTIL 1:45 P.M. SHARP TO GET READY, NOT wanting her to have too much time to ponder her next move.

After all, I had met Eric at his loft citing business reasons, but he had started to wise up that this was not business, but personal.

The fight in him was strong, but I was still stronger. He tried to scream as I tightened the belt around his neck. I picture him hanging, legs dangling in his closet, but moments before, I'd forced him to write a suicide note to his family, such a sweet gesture if you ask me.

He apologized for his affair, for tearing up a family, and for being gay.

Eric refused to write it until I showed him the gun Mark's wife had provided me. It was fitting that the gun belonged to Mark, his lover. Her intentions matched mine, but a gun was too risky, bullet casings too traceable. Though I thought about having it look like Mark had killed him, there were too many complications.

Levin needs to calm down, so I slip a couple of Xanax in a glass of white wine and bring it to her. The white wine won't stain her dress if she spills. By the way her hands shake, these little pills will be a welcome relief.

If she's comatose, she'll be less likely to cause a scene.

Her vows were a concern. I scratch my chin, not in the mood to kill her on our special day. I don't want our wedding to end with my beloved departing and all of this having been for nothing.

I prayed she did not make the same mistake Eric had. When he had put the pen to the paper and started writing, he had tried to write in the middle of the note that this wasn't a suicide. I had ripped it up and made him start again.

It had fueled my anger even more, and I had no problem yanking his head back and tightening the belt notch by notch. It was a quick death, eyes bulging out of his head, body hanging limp. He was half-naked, boxer briefs on, his apartment spotless except for his lifeless body.

I knock on the door with a glass of wine in hand.

I hear rustling and then footsteps as she walks across the room. "Are you ready?"

Her face looks a hundred times better, the makeup covering the unsettling parts. Thank God. No one wants to look at ugly marks on a pretty face.

"Yes."

"Vows written?" I ask.

"Yes."

"Okay, you can come out now." I step back and let her exit the room.

Even with a split lip and a bruised cheek, she looks stunning. She didn't need a hair stylist or a makeup artist. She managed fine on her own. Her hair was pulled back into a chignon, her eyes made up with a touch of eyeshadow and mascara, and her eyes were lined with charcoal eyeliner.

She kept her lips fairly neutral with light lipstick and some gloss.

I smile at her, a peace offering.

"Aren't you going to drink the wine?" I feign hurt. "Aren't most brides tipsy on their wedding day?"

She's considering the wine, probably wondering if I drugged it. "I don't want to smudge my lipstick." She's contrite as she takes a small sip.

My phone buzzes, and I reach into my pocket to answer it. I expect a call from George. The gate needs to be opened outside of the house since they have passed the guard entrance.

I press the code on my phone, then give Levin a warning look. "Don't disappoint me today. You look stunning. But you don't want to look stunning *dead*."

She is taken aback, and I grab her hand.

"The priest is here. It's time." I envelop her in my arms and kiss her pursed lips. I hold her hand, my grip firm.

A minute later, the doorbell rings, and I head that way unlatching the lock.

"Hello, George," I say as I open the double doors. "And Father Roberts. Thank you for coming on such short notice."

Father Roberts beams. "All my pleasure. I hear an elopement is in the cards today. What a beautiful view you have up here."

He lowers his voice. "I normally don't do weddings outside the church. George provided our parish with a *very* generous donation, and our congregation thanks you."

"I was so glad my friend let us borrow it for the weekend." I lead them into the house. "Please meet my lovely bride, Levin."

"Nice to meet you." Father Roberts shakes her hand, his

eyes kind and wrinkled. “My, you look like you just came out of a magazine.”

She thanks him saying nothing more.

As I introduce Levin to George, the color drains from her face.

I squeeze her hand, a warning to behave.

CHAPTER FORTY-THREE

LEVIN

"GEORGE," I SAY. MY SUSPICIONS WERE CORRECT ALL along. "I think we've met when I was at the resort. Oh, and CVS."

I can tell this is a man who rarely loses his composure. He recovers nicely, acknowledging me with a head nod.

He's dressed formally today—a suit and tie replace his cowboy boots and Wranglers. No chewing tobacco is visible in his mouth.

Father Roberts seems like a jovial individual, and I'm sorry this man of the cloth is an accomplice to a crime he didn't know was being committed.

As much as I try to match his mood, warning myself to act as a bride should act on her wedding day, the struggle is real. It's hard to be light-hearted and free-spirited instead of nauseous and anxious when you know you'll probably be in a body bag soon.

Father Roberts is adamant that a quick tour of the house

is a must. He's secretly impressed with the home, a sizeable difference from his quarters, he tells us.

"Is this your property or a rental?" Father Roberts asks.

Alec hesitates, not wanting to discuss any specifics in front of me. "It's a rental."

"Wow, what a place, I can't wait to see the rest."

"Yeah, it's quite the property. You saw the guard gate, it's like a *fortress* in here." He emphasizes the word, so I'll take the hint—I'm a prisoner in his castle.

"I noticed you aren't getting in without a good reason." Father Roberts winks at me. "You remind me of Rapunzel except without the 'being trapped' part."

There's a choking noise as Alec coughs, air getting trapped, and he reaches for his throat.

The irony in your sentence, Father Roberts, I think wryly.

"How about I get Father Roberts and George something to drink?" I play the good hostess card. If there is one pet peeve of Alec's, it's bad manners. You should always treat your guests like they're the center of attention when they're in your house.

Alec is attempting to put Father Roberts at ease, especially since small talk has never been his forte. He's wary of including me on the tour, so he asks George to accompany me to the kitchen.

"I'm good," George mutters as he fumbles through the kitchen cupboards looking for, I presume, a stiffer drink.

Father Roberts is wearing a white robe but has a briefcase in hand which he sets on the bar stool in the kitchen. I pretend not to notice as I walk over to the fridge, feeling the undeniable burn of Alec's eyes on my back as he enters the room.

"Look at this yard!" Father Roberts says looking out the window. "Perfect spot for your vows."

"Absolutely." Alec's voice drips with fake sincerity.

I bring glasses of sparkling water over to both Alec and Father Roberts as George busies himself in the kitchen making a vodka tonic.

I reach up and touch Alec's face adoringly, the scratches jagged in the light. He gives me a stilted smile before depositing a quick peck on my left cheek.

"Baby," Alec grabs my elbow. "How about I show Father Roberts where we intend to get married, and you entertain George?"

My hopes of being alone in the house while they explore quickly vanish. George is my keeper now. If I hadn't tried to escape earlier, I might have had an opportunity to be alone.

"Of course." I give him my biggest smile.

A quick glance at George shows he is watching my every move.

CHAPTER FORTY-FOUR

ALEC

THE HOUSE IS MASSIVE AND HAS MANY DEAD ENDS. HENCE, it is the perfect place to hold onto the things that belong to you. The entrance to the backyard is much further back since there isn't much room for a backyard because of the cliff.

The house was designed with the yard as a focal point, but there's only one way to get there. Once you were outside, you couldn't leave through any other manner. You're trapped.

There's a four-seasons room off of the bar which leads out to the backyard. It has floor-to-ceiling windows and encapsulates the magnificent views.

The patio is carved into the rock from the actual mountain. Patio chairs and green shrubbery with tall shrubs make you feel like you're in your own private sanctuary. The cacti are high enough to create a feeling of sheer isolation.

The infinity edge pool plays a trick on your eyes like it will cascade over the mountain as it stops right at the end.

The spa is built up higher, and water tumbles from the spa into the pool from various waterfalls.

A small patch of grass with a pergola is the ideal wedding spot.

I stop to show Father Roberts the yard pretending I know more about the house than I do. I tell him it's a friend's who rents it out during the peak season. It's exhausting, this forced interaction with people. I almost wish I had brought Levin with me, but I know she's in good hands with George.

Since it's our wedding day, I try to pay attention to the questions he's asking, but I'm nervous about Levin.

I don't have to worry long because, at that moment, George leads Levin outside.

"Thought she should help you with the wedding details." George has her by the arm, the red blotched skin apparent in the light of day.

I nod, as this makes the most sense. It does look suspicious if I'm the one taking care of all the details.

The priest is eyeing George and Levin, the way he grips her, the melancholy expression on her face. Demeanor says it all—the slumped shoulders, uneasy jaunt.

"Are you okay, honey?" His eyes are kind, presence calming.

They all look at her as she opens her mouth to speak. It's the moment of truth, and I'll deal with the repercussions of her actions.

CHAPTER FORTY-FIVE

LEVIN

NOW'S THE TIME, I CAN TELL THE PRIEST I'VE NO DESIRE TO be a bride.

I struggle to stay upright, my heels getting caught in the sod.

George guided me out here, my three-inch heels tripping over various steps. He blindfolded me, didn't want me to familiarize myself with my surroundings.

I think he gets a sick pleasure from watching me bump into walls and my obtuseness as I collide into what I presume to be a piece of furniture, the smell of pine filling my nostrils.

He doesn't take it off until we are outside away from the watchful eyes of the priest. And Alec.

All three sets of eyes bore into me.

"Father Roberts," I'm apologetic, "I have some concerns with my vows."

"Is that so?" he scratches his head. "This is common. It's

hard to put feelings into words and bottle love up in such a short timeframe."

I shift on my feet balancing from one foot to another.

George tightens his hold. My arm's a pin cushion for his nails as they dig into me.

"Is that your only issue?" The priest's observant gaze tries to hold mine. I look away. All I can do is shrug. I look around surveying the picturesque landscape.

I try not to make it obvious I'm searching, searching for any way off this damned mountain. Am I better suited to get Father Roberts' attention by whispering or passing him a note? My vows are tucked into the garter underneath my dress, as cheesy and over-the-top as I knew Alec liked.

The priest turns back to Alec, and I can tell from Alec's crossed arms and stilted conversation that he's uncomfortable in this forced and awkward situation, anxious to get started with the ceremony.

"George," the priest asks, "would you mind grabbing me a chair?"

"Of course," George and Alec exchange a quick glance, and then George releases my arm. He walks off to grab a patio chair.

Father Roberts reaches into his robe, his face mirroring his confusion as he looks around, consternation as he lays his hand on the bible he's holding.

"Dear," he says, eyes kind, "would you mind going in and grabbing my glasses? I believe I left them in the kitchen on the counter by the coffee maker."

"Absolutely," I try to keep the excitement out of my voice.

Alec hesitates, "I'll go get them. You stay here and tell Father Roberts what type of ceremony you envision."

"Okay," I show my teeth in a big smile. "I'll talk to Father Roberts about my vows, you go ahead." His face turns ashen as his mouth tightens. He looks around for George so I'm not left alone with the priest. "Why don't we just go in together?"

"Actually," Father Roberts claps him on the shoulder. "Mind if I talk to you alone for a second?"

I don't realize I'm holding my breath until I start to cough.

Alec is scanning the yard for George who has a chair in hand but is now on his cell. His animated voice carries over to us, but I can't understand him.

He wants to keep me close, but Father Roberts is already leading him closer to the pergola to talk ceremony details.

George turns his back to us, the phone cradled to his ear.

Running is an option, but not a good one. I don't look at Alec as I turn away, keeping my pace slow and steady as I start to head toward the door. I can at least find that. The wedding dress is heavy with beading and lace, and the shoes make my movements clunky.

As soon as I step out of sight, I pick up the pace. Father Roberts left his glasses, but did he have his cell phone?

My brain is amped up going a million miles a minute. Does this house have a landline? This might be my only opportunity to try for help, to get out of here alive and free.

George will be hot on my trail when he sees I went off alone.

I go to the left when I get inside and end up in the billiards room complete with a pool table and bar. The decor consists of cliché *Brat Pack* images and polished mahogany furniture.

Eyes darting, I see all windows but no doors in the room.

Seems to be the theme of this place.

I head down a narrow hallway, a large floor-to-ceiling mirror at the end, my reflection a sore sight. My wrists are covered with burn marks, and my face stares back at me, ghastly, the makeup heavy on my face. It matches the feeling in my heart.

The doors on either side lead into another bedroom with an en-suite bathroom and then a large study on the other side. It has a large oak desk with bookshelves filled with dated encyclopedias and detective fiction. It doesn't look like Alec has ever used this room, everything is neat and tidy.

My nerves are shot as I reverse direction and proceed the way I came. I consider hiding but the house is too spread out, and I don't want to be stuck without any access or ability to find the front door which seems to be the only way out.

My heels reverberate on the tile floor as I start down another hallway coming upon a large dining area with a two-sided fireplace that looks into the great room. The kitchen is beyond that. I see the black and white tiled floor and the stainless steel appliances. I want to sink down in relief, but I know this is the moment I've been waiting for.

It takes me a few dead ends to find the kitchen from this part of the house. I try to slow my breathing, reminding myself that escape is imminent, that I'm close to being free.

The reading glasses aren't on the counter. I find them in his briefcase. I dip my hand in the front pouch, hoping to feel my fingertips graze a glass phone screen.

Nothing.

My heart sinks as the rest of the pockets are empty. I reach into the briefcase, one of the compartments has an object at the bottom.

Jackpot.

A flip phone rests inside the right pocket, large and clumsy, one that most likely came from the starting era of technology. It is even older than my basic burner phone.

I punch in 911, let it ring, and say, "Emergency" into the phone and hang up. I can't risk Alec seeing me on the phone. He'd kill us all.

Since the advancement of cell phone technology made landlines and even phone calls, obsolete, I didn't have anyone's number memorized.

I wish I knew Amada's by heart. Maddy's too far away. Or hell, even Jake's.

With no other options, I send a text to my work cell phone. It had been in Jake's villa when I was snatched. I had accidentally left it in his walk-in when I was going through his suits. If my memory served me, it's on the floor, hopefully not kicked into a pile of clothing.

My hunch told me Alec would've grabbed my personal cell since it was near the bathtub when I was kidnapped.

I wasn't sure it if was even working at this point. Alec could have destroyed it, or the battery could be drained by now.

All I knew was that I couldn't risk Alec seeing me on this phone. He would kill me with his bare hands.

My instinct says not to keep the phone on me. Alec will find it. I briskly open one of the cabinet doors and hide the phone in a spaghetti pot, careful to keep the metal from clanging as it falls into the metal bottom. I slam the door shut just as Alec enters the room, relief palpable on his face as he realizes I'm still here.

"Did you find the glasses?" There's an edge to his voice. He doesn't like that I've been out of his sight for this long.

I nod and start to walk past him. He seizes me and pushes me up against the counter.

"What else did you find?" He snarls, his face inches from mine. He reminds me of a rabid dog, teeth bared, ready to pounce.

He jerks my head back, and I gasp in shock before he pulls my head forward and releases me.

I stare up at him, his eyes black slits.

"Nothing," I speak neutral, my eyes level with his as I keep my voice even, the terror inside threatening to grab my insides and twist until I lose all composure.

He releases me and grabs the briefcase searching the pockets. All he comes up with is a piece of tissue and some scraps of paper. My heart skips a beat.

Was the address of the property on one of those pieces?

"Let's go." He pushes me ahead of him. He carries the briefcase with him. "I'm going to bring this outside. I don't want any more surprises."

We are halfway down the hallway, when a phone rings, the tone shrill and unexpected.

Alec touches his pocket, then glares at me. I shrug my shoulders.

He hooks me around the waist and pulls me forcibly back toward him.

The ringing continues.

His hands are rough as he manhandles me searching furiously for any sign of a phone on my body. "You better not have a phone, bitch." He warns, his fingers harsh to the touch as he lifts my dress up and touches my crevices for proof that I am not carrying any contraband.

He feels the paper in my garter and tears it out, ripping the vows in half.

"Oh..." He's chastened as he looks at the scraps in his hand. "Sorry, doll. I didn't realize you put them there." His voice softens, and he takes my hand, caressing it this time instead of yanking it.

We head back to the kitchen, Alec unconvinced that it's not on me by the way he keeps darting his eyes up and down my body.

I pray the phone stops ringing, or he will be able to find it.

Alec is a madman, tearing around the kitchen, opening drawers, pulling open cabinets. There is a lid on the pot I threw it in, so it is unseen by the naked eye.

A loud beep commences signaling a message.

The priest walks in at that moment to see Alec's meltdown, a child in an adult body, throwing a tantrum. He is speechless as he stares between the two of us. He didn't know Alec 3.0.

"Is everything okay?" The priest's concerned, his tone soothing. "Do we need to take a minute?"

Alec waits until George enters the room and storms out, a curt nod toward me exchanged, thrusting the briefcase into George's arms.

The beep resounds again.

"Sounds like I have a message." The priest carries the briefcase over to the counter.

I'm glued to the spot, wanting to sink through the tile. I move forward to hand him his glasses. It's amazing they aren't broken considering Alec's manhandling of me.

"Thanks, dear." He slides them on his face and unzips his bag.

He rummages around unable to locate his phone.

"Hmm," he's confused. "I don't know where my phone is."

George is staring at me, his jaw set in a hard line.

The priest looks between us.

"Have either of you seen my phone?"

I shake my head making sure to keep eye contact with him.

"Do you know where it is?" The priest's voice is low, but there's a pressing urgency in his tone.

My eyes plead with his, silently begging him to drop it.

He reaches back into the front pocket. "Phew," he says, pretending to feel something in the bottom. He looks up at both of us, "I'm getting old and losing my mind."

George is placated though he's waiting for him to pull the phone out.

"George," Alec's yelling from down the hall, his voice echoing. "Take five."

CHAPTER FORTY-SIX

ALEC

I DECIDE TO GO INTO THE STUDY TO CHECK LEVIN'S PHONE. I am skittish about it being traced, so it has been turned off and locked in a desk drawer.

My journal is next to it, as I'm still writing out my thoughts.

I want to remember every detail of today—the wedding dress, the way she looked, the ceremony, and our vows.

This is my tribute to Levin. Instead of keeping a lock of hair or a locket like I did with Heidi, I keep a history of her.

The key is still in its same place tucked under a large oriental rug in the study, the wood floors covered by the massive gray monstrosity, the pattern of shapes an eyesore. I bend down under one of the corners and pull it out, the small metal key shines against the gloss of the floor.

I sink down into the leather chair in front of the desk reaching my hand out to stick the key into the lock.

The desk drawer squeaks in protest as I wrench it open. It's lying face down on the black moleskin, dead to the world.

It's off.

I flip the cover of the phone open and press the 'ON' button. The urge to know if Levin contacted her phone is eating at me. I have to know if she got to a phone.

There're multiple text messages and calls. I thumb through the history. Nothing alarming. I chuckle to myself. I mean, a lot of distressing voicemails from others, but nothing a few minutes ago.

Might as well delete all of these. Some of the names I don't recognize.

A Maddy? Amada? I recognize the trainer's voice calling again. A headache is brewing. I start humming to try to calm myself, the brink of disaster narrowly averted.

I rest my head on the desk shutting my eyes against the cool wood.

My mind drifts to killing her. The dress ethereal, a perfect funeral gown.

Levin would look as peaceful in a coffin. I sit up suddenly.

A wicked grin forms as I lean back in the chair, the leather crinkling underneath me as I picture her silent and still, her hair framing her features, though it might have to be a closed casket.

Or they can put a high-collar dress on her to cover up the purple.

No longer able to cause me pain and suffering.

Leaving me a rich man.

CHAPTER FORTY-SEVEN

Levin

We give Alec his five minutes of peace, whatever that means.

George is feeling me out looking me up and down, his creepy gaze undressing me until I'm virtually naked.

I ignore his salacious eyes and make my way toward Father Roberts.

"Oh Father, Alec's just nervous. Me, too. It's such a big day for us." If George hadn't lifted his shirt a minute ago and pointed to the gun in his holster, I'd be screaming for help instead of pretending nothing's wrong.

I roll my eyes, my fear not going to get the best of me with that jackass.

Father Roberts is unaware of this exchange and nods in agreement. "It certainly is. You are committing yourself to each other before God. It's not to be taken lightly."

Alec strides back in the room, his confidence back, his head raised like a peacock.

There's a perma-smile stuck on his face.

I stare out the kitchen window taking deep breaths.

I don't want to be near him, and I desperately need us to get outside before the phone beeps again.

My last-ditch attempt is to grasp Father Roberts' hand and say, "Let's go outside, I'm ready to be Alec's wife."

Alec pulls his phone out of his pocket. He scrolls down, and as we head outside, he shows me a picture of last night—me tied up, passed out, him pretending to gut me with a knife.

It's pressed into my skin almost piercing it.

That's when I notice Alec's body, blood coming out of a wound.

My eyes widen as I realize it's my initials carved into his skin.

He's looking for a reaction, a sick, twisted smile on his face.

I'm not going to give him the pleasure.

I keep my eyes straight ahead swallowing the fear I feel.

CHAPTER FORTY-EIGHT

ALEC

I DIDN'T WANT EITHER OF THEM OUT OF MY SIGHT.

We head back outside to get married. Levin's engagement ring is in my pocket nestled beside the wedding band I've purchased, both burning a hole.

I want nothing more than for this disaster to be over with and fast.

Houdini couldn't make Father Roberts disappear fast enough. I want Levin to myself. If I have to hide her for the next nine months, I will keep her in seclusion.

We're going to start working on that baby tonight, I decide. And we're going to keep trying until her belly is swollen with my child.

Then... as soon as she has the baby, I'm killing her.

Our gallant wedding party, if you can call it that, steps back outside to exchange vows. George is standing up as the required witness.

We take our places in front of the priest. George does double duty as the unofficial wedding photographer.

Father Roberts begins with an opening prayer. We're on our way to man and wife. When we get to our vows, I read mine. They're memorized, but I still need reminders, so I retrieve the folded slip of paper from my left breast pocket.

I promise to cherish her, love her, and treasure her... until the day she dies. I focus on the words, intent on her reaction as I promise until death do us part.

And I mean every word.

CHAPTER FORTY-NINE

LEVIN

A MAN WHO'S STALKING ME IS THE WITNESS AT MY wedding to a cold-blooded killer. This would make for good reality TV. Isn't there a show called my 'Crazy Ex' on *Lifetime*? This scenario would take the cake, literally and figuratively.

My dress is itchy on my skin, and it takes all my concentration not to scratch at it—the feeling of ants crawling underneath the surface a very real sensation at the present moment.

Father Roberts is reading passages, and I divert my attention between my sensitive skin and the text and phone call I made to 911. By some miracle, does Jake have my phone? Does he think I just left? No, he wouldn't. He knew I felt like I was in danger. There had to have been a puddle of water on the floor from the tub.

I finger the small tears in the dress where Alec had clawed at me in the kitchen. I'm despondent thinking that no one knows where I am.

All these people knew I was on the run, but no one knew to look for me.

My only hope is that the resort is suspicious since I didn't show up for my shift. They might think I'm flaky or didn't take work seriously, but Amada would tell them. She would also alert Maddy. Jake presumably would also be concerned. He might think I left town since my stuff left with me.

Maybe water was left in the tub, and it raised the level of alarm?

Could I get the phone and try 911 again or check to see if my text had gone through?

I thought someone had answered the 911 call before I hung up, but now that I think about it, all I heard was static.

My panic rises as I grasp the reality that I might be stuck with Alec after the ceremony and what that means.

I might not be dead today, or tonight, but I was dead.

There's no way in hell Alec is keeping me around. He wants the money.

If we marry, and I die, it goes to him.

The priest turns to me and smiles. "Levin, do you have anything you want to say?"

"Yes, Father Roberts." I take a deep breath. "I don't want to marry him. Not today, not ever."

The stunned look on Alec's face is replaced by hatred.

His blind rage is apparent, but I figure my chances with two witnesses, albeit one a priest and one an accomplice, are better than none.

After the ceremony, I'll be stuck alone with Alec, tortured, most certainly raped, then killed.

Father Roberts searches my face for a sign that I'm being facetious or even kidding. But the fear in my eyes and dilated pupils tell a different story.

"Let's give the lady some time to breathe." He puts down his bible.

Alec fakes a smile. "Let's step away a second." He's pulling me out of earshot. He keeps it plastered on and whispers under his breath, "You stupid bitch. I should've killed you when I had the chance. If you go back inside or try to get help, I'll fucking strangle you the way I strangled your dear friend."

I burn holes into Alec as I stare at him, then I turn back to Father Roberts.

The last thing I want is to get Father Roberts hurt. I know what Alec is capable of and with George, there's no telling what they would do. I doubt that he's excused from Alec's wrath just because he's a man of God.

I weight my options. George has a gun. Alec has a knife. They have the control.

But I have the money.

I place my bets and roll the dice.

"Let's go," I say to him. "Please, let's go now. I'm being held against my will."

Once more he looks at me, unsure how to respond, an uncomfortable silence follows. I can tell he's concerned but doesn't know me or what to do at this point.

"Why don't we go inside, and we can discuss this?" Father Roberts is agonized after my outburst. He's rubbing his hands together as if he can wash away the unease.

He's at an impasse—his duty is to officiate a wedding, not a funeral. And I imagine the last thing he expected when he arrived today was to be walking into a crime scene.

I start to follow the priest, but Alec pulls me to the side, his grip on my arm matches his tone. The priest is now further ahead of me out of earshot.

Alec takes the opportunity to wrap his hands around my neck cutting off my circulation.

"You're going to finish your vows without one more

outburst, do you understand?" I can't even open my mouth to respond. "Or this will be the last breath you take."

I'm gasping, choking for air, as he squeezes, intent on sucking the air out of my lungs.

I'm dead, vows or not. He'll kill me now or later.

"You're going to apologize to Father Roberts, say this is a bad joke." He's grasping his ear as he lets go of me.

I want to scream for the priest, but George makes sure to keep him occupied, their voices hushed ahead of us. He hasn't the slightest clue what's going on.

So close but so far away.

CHAPTER FIFTY

ALEC

THE BITCH IS GOING TO DIE. I'M GOING TO CHOKE HER out, and her last memory will be of my face haunting her.

My vision is red, and it's impeding everything, a shade that makes my mood, well, murderous.

Levin tried to give me up. How dare she?

No one knew she was missing. The house, or mansion, to put it accurately, is carved into the side of the mountain like it's a natural formation that appeared as part of the landscape.

There's no numbering on the structure or any signage which helps my case.

No one can find us without specific instructions. A gate code. The guard calling me.

But what now that we've been seen by the priest?

At this point, forging marriage documents and going back to California might be preferable. I'm sure George knows someone who could help with that. And Levin could be dead after they're signed.

There's an expression of horror, not bridal bliss, on her face, a variance from the typical bride.

Regretting my quick instinct to choke her, I unclench my hands from her throat.

The knife's still in my pocket. I had it just in case she didn't behave.

I whisper in her ear and shove it in the small of her back at the same time, "It's time to make a deal."

She opens her mouth to speak but still hasn't caught her breath. It's all air.

I press the knife harder into her skin. "Don't play dumb."

There's a low whisper, "If you're going to kill me, what does it matter?"

"I won't kill you if you marry me. I need the money."

"I don't believe you," her mouth's in a hard line. "You'll just kill me later on."

I'm desperate. Levin motions that she needs to sit down. I lead her to the edge of the cliff, a downward fall the only way to escape.

"What're the terms?" She's spent, her voice emotionless.

"Marry me. Have children with me." I wave the knife around in the air.

"But why wouldn't I marry someone I love?" She's disgusted at my proposal. "You'll kill me the first chance you get. You do realize you won't get the money?" She's disgusted. "The kids have to be eighteen before they see a dime."

I shake my head. George can take care of that. Forging is a loose term.

"I love you, though," I plead. "We can make a deal."

My resolve's melting. I don't want to kill her. I want to stop this precipitous behavior. I vow to stop hurting what's mine.

"Who is that man at the villa?" I change topics.

"I never cheated on you, Alec." She sighs.

"Who he is?" I trace the dirt with my shoe, the patent leather a dusty tan now, matching the desert backdrop.

"A guest of the resort, nothing more." Her lips are pursed in thought.

Enough about that sorry bastard.

"Marry me, Levin." I get back on track with the knife still poised in her lower back.

"Put the knife away, Alec." She tries to turn her body away from my grip on her.

"Then tell me what I want to hear."

"I can't marry you." Tears are streaming down her face. "You killed Eric."

My face twists into a grimace, the earlier façade crackling.

"How dare you?" I bellow.

With the truth hanging in the air, I have to get rid of her and get rid of her now. There's no turning back.

I seize her by the nape of the neck and walk toward the edge, the knife now cutting into her skin.

Levin starts screaming, but I clap a hand over her mouth.

She tries to spin around and sink her teeth into my hand at the same time.

I shriek and slap her across the face.

Behind me, someone hollers.

Startled, she falls backward.

Everything is happening in slow-motion as Levin goes down disappearing from sight.

I turn around in time to see the frozen look on a man's face.

He's tall, and the way he carries himself looks familiar.

As he gets closer, I see the CEO of that solar energy company, Jake Hunter, appear in my view.

I'm aghast that he's here witnessing this. I'm right, she's a cheating whore. This is her flavor of the week.

My focus should be on Levin, but the audacity of this man to show up on *my* wedding day, of all days, to snatch my bride from me, makes me want to hurdle myself at him punching him in the gut. One more person to get rid of, I sigh.

Oh, Levin darling, you're free to explore your new choice in men.

Too bad you'll be dead.

There's a blood-curdling scream as Levin tumbles down. Along with Jake, I hear the squawk of Father Roberts, a rasping sound.

And two policemen.

I hold up my knife to let them know they're not going to hurt me.

They sprint past me and almost lose their balance on the edge as they skid to a stop.

They look down horrified to see it's too late.

She's gone.

CHAPTER FIFTY-ONE

LEVIN

THERE'S A GUTTURAL SCREAM, AND IT'S UNCLEAR IF IT'S coming from one of the men above or me.

I recognize the police uniforms and standing in between the two is Jake.

His outline stands out against the rest of the world—brown hair, piercing eyes, and at this very second, the deer-in-the-headlights expression as he realizes what's happening.

I'll never forget that look as long as I live, the numb horror on his face.

I hit my head as I connect with a sharp rock. Everything blurs.

Somehow, as I'm tumbling down, I manage to grab a handful of weeds growing out of the soil in between some boulders.

I feel the blood gush out of a wound on my head as I try to hold myself steady from sliding backward. If I hit the next drop, it will be my last breath. Alec won't even get the satisfaction of doing me in.

I'm gasping for air trying to see through the trickling stream of blood that's running down my eye. The weeds are breaking apart in my hand disconnecting from their roots. My fingers make an effort to dig into the soil, but it's rocky and clay-like, compliments of the desert.

I take another deep breath, my hand losing the last bit of grip it has.

My thoughts drift to Jake—unsatisfied this is our ending. But at least he knows what happened to me. They will find my body. Before it was questionable. I could be buried in the desert, body parts hidden under a rock somewhere, discovered during the next ice age.

There's nothing left to hold onto, nothing else in my visual horizon.

Only one way down, and I'm headed straight for it.

My eyes close in anticipation of the unknown. I brace for impact.

CHAPTER FIFTY-TWO

ALEC

I HOLD ON TO THE KNIFE CLUTCHING IT IN MY HAND LIKE it's my lifeline.

Jake's there in an instant, trying to find a way down that results in Levin being saved.

I'm pleased with my timeliness, the perfect end to a fucking nightmare. He sees her die. It's worth it even though it wasn't technically at my hands.

I'm concerned about the priest witnessing this. George is going to have another job to do. I hate to mess with clergy, but desperate times call for extreme measures.

Jake starts to inch forward and crawl down the side as the other men grab his legs. They ignore me for the present moment, all hands on Levin's removal from the mountain.

Hopefully, dead on arrival.

A police officer comes running over with the bungee cord and rope they must've found in my stash.

It was never intended to save a life, just imprison one.

Working together, they're able to tie some of the ropes together and secure the bungee cord on an impenetrable rock.

Disbelief clouds my face as my eyes twitch, my ears ring, dumbfounded that my chance to kill the crazy bitch is being sidetracked.

This isn't supposed to turn into a rescue mission.

She deserves to be thrown down to her demise for all the hell she's put me through.

"George," I scream. "Shoot her." I stamp my feet jumping up and down. I wave the knife around, "Kill her *now*."

He's in shock, his impenetrable façade starting to crumble. He turns and runs toward the house, this well-planned kidnapping a nightmare.

I'm frantic, my life and its trajectory flashing before my eyes—Eric, Heidi, my parents, Levin, the money.

She's too much trouble, I think.

No good deed goes unpunished, and it certainly hadn't in this case.

Levin's had a good life since she met me, the stability she had craved.

She couldn't handle it.

How can someone be so self-absorbed that they don't see they've been afforded every opportunity to have a privileged lifestyle?

My God, I think, she grew up without two nickels to rub together.

She meets me, and I change her life. All for the better. Clothes. Shoes. Furniture.

I made it possible for her to be unemployed, to have a killer body, and left the door open for plastic surgery. All I asked for in return is that she realize her place, that she belongs to me. The questions needed to cease.

She inherits money, and after all I do for her, she doesn't think I'm entitled to some.

Ungrateful bitch.

She's treated me like shit, raked me over the coals, battled me at every turn.

Just like everyone else—only into herself.

I would've confided in her about the business woes, eventually, but what good would that have done?

Eric's dead. I had made that an absolute.

CHAPTER FIFTY-THREE

LEVIN

I'M STUNNED. I OPEN MY EYES, AND JAKE'S RIGHT IN FRONT of me instead of standing at the top.

I feel like he's a mirage, the sun creating a surreal larger-than-life man.

I shut them again and quickly open them. He's still standing there, just closer now.

The feeling of solace overwhelms me. He's here. I was starting to think I'd never see him again. I'm beyond delighted.

We lock eyes, and he grabs my hand wincing at the cuts and bruises on my wrist, the ugly red marks a sordid reminder of the last day.

Nothing is said. There's no time to waste.

He instructs me to grab the rope he's clutching in his hand.

My vision's blurred, the blood congealed, but I'm able to

hold on as all three men pull the rope back, fast and in quick succession, getting Jake and me back on solid footing.

As soon as Jake can reach for my arm, he does.

The look of relief as I'm pulled up onto the ground is unmistakable.

I frantically search for Alec.

He's off to the side, still holding the knife, the sunlight glinting off it.

"He's got a knife, watch out," I scream.

Now that the men are satisfied I'm safe, they turn their attention toward Alec.

Alec, in a cowardly act, takes off running. The police officers remove their guns from their holsters and follow suit.

Jake doesn't leave my side, but sits back on the edge of a large rock and scoots back pulling me into his lap. My dress is tattered, shards of rock caught the fabric along with prickly bushes, maybe even a cactus, and long slits made a jagged pattern across it.

My heels fell off on the way down when I lost my footing, and my face is a swollen mess. A bruise is on one cheek, and now there's a wicked cut that's going to require some medical attention. I still had my limbs intact, and I am alive.

The rest of my body is scratched up and sore, yet the reassurance that Jake's beside me is enough to overcome the superficial wounds.

Jake holds me as close as he physically can wrap me up in his arms. I breathe in his expensive cologne mixed with dry, desert air which will forever be the scent of comfort and relief.

He examines my face and arms before I bury it in his broad chest, and his somber face is enough to bring tears to my eyes.

There's so much to say, yet, there's nothing.

The silence spans on as the sobs wrack my body, and he

pulls me closer soothing me with kind words and rubbing my back.

I don't want to move from his embrace.

He brings his head in close to my face, and I feel wetness, his tears mixing with mine.

"Levin," he breathes into my ear. "Levin, I thought I had..." There's no need to continue the sentence, the gravity of what could've been is known between us.

The brown eyes are a deep chocolate color today. They peer deep into my eyes, and I'm privy to his emotions, a raw energy that's brought him here—determination.

"How did you find me?" I sound tired. "Was it the text I sent?"

He shakes his head, "Nope, it couldn't be traced. But the police were able to get access to your friend in San Diego. When you weren't at the villa, I contacted your supervisors. The woman whose name starts with an 'A'?"

"Amada, yes, Maddy's cousin."

"She got in touch with Maddy and explained your situation." Jake touches my skin, a night and day difference from Alec's roughness. "We thought..." He can't finish his sentence, he gulps.

"Another woman had also contacted the police. A woman named Janice."

"Who's George?" I'm curious. "I mean, what's his relation to Alec?"

"He's former military, former cop." Jake's thumbing my cheek. "He's a PI now."

"That explains a lot." I'm putting together the pieces of how Alec has had his chum follow me, keep tabs on me, and is here for support.

"What is this place?" I whisper.

"A huge house. It's not far from the resort. Just up higher

and heavily guarded." Jake sighs. "It took us some maneuvering to get in here and find the place."

"How did you find the place?"

"There was an email from Alec to the owner. He paid for this place in cash and was careful not to leave paper trails. However, he emailed the owner about early checkout."

"Meaning?"

"Meaning he wanted to leave today instead of keeping it for another few days." Jake pulls me close. "We lucked out. He just sent the email this morning. The cops have been watching his email communications. It's been nil. His cell is also not picking up a signal."

I absorb this information for a minute, then it hits me—I was going to be dead. He was going to head home, go back to our life in San Diego, and I was slated for an early departure on life.

"They were able to track his movements over the last few days, and they found the church the priest came from."

I'm monotone as I say, "He killed my best friend, Eric, and his ex-girlfriend."

Jake's look is one of horror as he rubs my neck and nuzzles me to him. "We'll have to tell the police. And one day, I'd like to hear about your best friend."

Jake's trying to snap me out of my thoughts and the gravity of this moment.

He reaches for my mouth and kisses me gently on one side, careful to avoid my wound, then one on my forehead, the very best kind—soft and gentle yet possessive, protective.

The sound of a gunshot rings out, and Jake makes a quick move to make sure his body covers mine.

"Jake," I plead. "Please don't leave me."

The thought of him leaving me right now makes me shake. I instinctively tilt into his body, trying to protect myself using him as a shield.

He puts his finger in front of his lips, motioning me to be quiet.

"I know you're traumatized, but I need you to crawl. Can you do that?" Jake brushes his hand over my face.

I shake my head. My energy is tapped out. I can't speak.

We start to crawl around the side of the pool, though there's not much foliage to hide behind, the shrubs the only source of protection.

"Levin," Jake kisses my forehead, "I need to see what's going on and how we can get out of here. I need you to stay ducked down behind this bush."

I start to open my mouth, but the look he gives me changes my mind. He kneads his fingers through mine before stroking my hair and giving me a look, an unspoken promise he'll come back for me.

This is survival. Alec has a knife, George has a gun, and there have been gunshots.

CHAPTER FIFTY-FOUR

ALEC

I RAN FOR MY LIFE. I RAN FOR MY FREEDOM.

Was an escape even possible?

Inside the house, I didn't get far. I made it to the bedroom where my wallet's stashed and am barricaded by the two officers.

The cops ask me to sit down, weapons drawn.

It's not a choice.

They read me my Miranda rights.

The priest is stunned, his ceremony an apparent murder plot. He holds his bible in hand, head bowed.

Even though he had no prior inkling of the plot, he's ashamed to be roped into this.

Is there a way to convince him to lie for me?

There can't be enough evidence to convict me of a crime. I just took her for a little while. Borrowed, I would say. She *is* my fiancée.

George sits down beside me on the bed. Silent. Stoic. His usual demeanor.

I don't know what the cops have on me.

For all they know, this is just a domestic incident. A fight that went awry.

Officer Talladega, as I call him, based on his heavy Southern drawl, has long legs and spidery arms, and starts to ask me questions.

He wants to know about Levin, her disappearance, why we're in this house, what happened in San Diego, our relationship.

Everything's bubbling to the surface, the tsunami of emotions rising—anger and deception—as I clasp my hands in my lap.

He continues on about Levin's condo. Why she's in Arizona. Why I'm in Arizona.

I don't answer any questions. I want my attorney present.

The cops are annoyed, but they have to follow procedure.

The only answers I want to know are why Jake Hunter is here and what his relationship is to my fiancée.

Who the fuck knows?

I've always outshined and outsold a lie better than anyone —a mix of smooth and calm confidence paired with direct eye contact. This time, it's not working.

Officer Talladega's partner, a larger Hispanic fellow who's thirty pounds overweight and sweating profusely in his uniform, advises me that I'm under arrest for the kidnapping of Levin Crowdley.

That's when I hop up shoving Talladega off guard and attempt to grab his weapon.

His friend, the stooge, grabs his gun in one swift movement, not what I would expect from someone his size and aims at me.

He misses any vital organs but still manages to shoot me in the arm.

They pull me and drag me out to the living room and radio in for backup.

CHAPTER FIFTY-FIVE

LEVIN

I'M INCONSOLABLE LAYING UNDERNEATH THE BUSH, MY body a wreck, my heart pumping furiously, and the adrenaline rush coming on full-force.

Jake's heading back inside, and his unknown whereabouts since he is out of my line of vision is killing me.

I'm not ready to be alone yet.

After I hear a shot fired, I sit up, alert, waiting for any sign of the police officers, the priest, George, or Jake.

Such an interesting mix for a wedding.

All we needed is the cast of the Village People, and suddenly we'd have a party.

I chuckle to myself wondering how the hell I managed to have a sense of humor amidst everything that's just taken place, but it doesn't matter. My emotions have already run the full gamut today.

But my light moment is cut short by the sharp throb of my eye. It's beginning to swell, closing shut.

My instinct is to run in the direction of the gunshot, but I'm hurt. The rampant desire to know what's going down is driving me nuts, my blood pressure is through the roof, but Jake told me to stay here, and I trust him.

The seconds tick by, although I could swear they're hours. I'm haunted by the fear that something bad is going to happen at the hands of George or Alec.

I'm focused intently on what I can see of the house, which isn't much, and my nerves are on high alert. Someone is striding toward me, and my instinct is to run. I shut my eyes, willing the pounding in my head to stop.

I make out his form. It's familiar.

He's coming back to finish me off.

Except it's Jake. I smell the cologne—a familiar scent—it lingers in the air. I can breathe.

When he reaches me, he doesn't say a word but just carefully picks me up in his arms as if I'm weightless. I wrap my arms around his neck, inhaling his scent, the cologne mixed with sweat, as he carries me into the house.

The great room has been turned into a crime scene. There're couch cushions strewn on the floor, and Alec's arm is bleeding profusely onto a towel. He's sitting on the cushions on the floor and leaning his head back against the couch.

I've never seen Alec defeated until today, handcuffs on his wrists, blanket covering his arm, a make-shift tourniquet to stop the bleeding.

I want to feel elated inside, but all I can muster is pity.

I remind myself that he's the evil one. He made his bed. Now he can sleep in it—preferably in a jail cell.

The officers are waiting for the ambulance to arrive.

My body shudders when I spot him, and I bury my head in Jake's shoulder. He strides through the hallway at a fast clip until we arrive in the kitchen. He delicately sets me down on an overstuffed loveseat in the corner next to another fireplace, this one is wood-burning.

He sits down beside me, his arm wrapped tight around my waist.

I rest my head on his chest, closing my eyes to today's events wanting nothing more than to wake up, well-rested like Sleeping Beauty—this all a horrible nightmare.

As the cops search the house, they find Alec's laptop in a case. Some papers were shoved into a pocket, and they pulled them out.

One of the officers mentions Eric's name, and my ears perk up.

Curious to see what he found, he shows me the papers.

Eric McGrath's final will had left his business interests to a Ms. Levin Crowdley or next of kin.

The company they founded, EMAW Real Estate Holdings, had belonged to both Eric and Alec. Eric had the majority stake—ninety percent—whereas Alec had only ten percent.

I was the golden ticket as he stood to inherit everything if we got married or had children.

The cops confiscate the papers as evidence, and I sit, awestruck, as I reflect on how close I came to being another one of his victims.

"Will you find my purse?" I ask. The idea of walking through a room and staring Alec in the face is too overwhelming.

"Sure." He gives me a gentle squeeze and slowly stands up. "Any idea where it is?"

"I think one of the bedrooms," I shrug my shoulders, "or in a bathroom."

Jake is only gone for a few minutes before he comes back with the tan leather handbag. There's a scrap of paper in his hand.

I tilt my head in wonder.

He hands it to me. It's the note I had written and tucked into the corner of the bed underneath the duvet cover. It was written in tiny handwriting, such big thoughts in a condensed space.

Jake's feeble as he reads that I've been kidnapped and now am probably dead.

The reality of what might've been sets in for him.

We were at least a hundred feet apart, but he covered those steps in seconds as if there was no distance between us.

He reaches for me and envelops my tired body grounding me with his weight.

We hear the paramedics come, and Jake goes to watch them take Alec away, his arm hanging limply at his side in his cuffs, reassurance he is no longer a danger.

I'm perched on the loveseat unable to move, my strength drained.

Jake went to answer a couple of questions, and he's promised to get me as soon as the other ambulance arrives. He can tell I need a minute to process.

"He's gone," Jake says as he comes into the kitchen nook. "They took him away."

Jake helps me stand and leads me back to the great room now cleared out except for one officer and one paramedic.

Father Roberts had left with the other officer and paramedic. He's going to head to the station to give his statement on how he'd come in contact with Alec. George has vanished, though the officer assures me he's in cuffs and headed down to the station. He'd been found walking down the mountain road when he was picked up by the authorities.

The female paramedic guides me into a bedroom and asks me to remove my clothing.

There isn't much left of this dress, the shreds a glaring

reminder of Alec. I tremble as I undress, the unease still overtaking me.

I have mainly superficial cuts on my body, though my forehead is going to need some stitches.

There's a knock at the door. It's Jake holding my ratty robe. I have no idea how he thought to bring it.

"I thought you could use this." He eases me into it.

He stays by my side while they suture my face and put Vaseline on the contusions.

The police ask if I'm okay to talk to them. I'm ready. Finally.

Now is the time to unburden myself with Eric and his death. Heidi, I can describe, but her family and friends will have to provide the specifics.

I offer to show them the note Eric left me. The fake suicide note.

We agree to meet at the condo where I can retrace the steps of the last year, beginning to end, and then some.

BACK AT THE CONDO, SOME OF THE QUESTIONS ARE BRUTAL, and so much is like ripping off a Band-Aid and dredging up old wounds. After the next few hours, I might need to sleep for a year.

"Hi, I'm Officer Frost," a Hispanic-woman who barely reaches five feet has been sent to interview me. "This is Officer Cooper." She points to her partner in crime. He's short and stocky, a middle-aged man with very tan skin, and the wrinkles to prove it.

We sit around the living room as if we're at a Tupperware party, each looking at the other, unsure of how to begin.

Officer Frost starts. "I know you've just been through a traumatic ordeal, but we'd like to get your statement."

Cooper jumps in, "We'd like to record it as well as take notes." He turns on his recorder, "Do we have your permission.

"Yes." I nod.

I'm curled up under a blanket on the couch, Jake sitting next to me, holding my hand.

He squeezes it tight as they begin their questions, recording my answers, my voice a mixture of hurt, anger, frustration, tears, and uncertainty at times as I try and speak to Alec's behavior. I know his motives for wanting to kill me, but did someone leaving him have that big of an effect on his ego?

It must, but it's still a level of psychology I don't understand. When the officers ask a tough question or prod, Jake goes into protective mode stroking my hair, tracing his finger on my palm, his eyes never leaving my face.

He can tell I'm exhausted—the day's events have turned into night, and I yawn, my eyes shutting for a moment.

"Can we wrap this up?" Jake is back in his take-charge mode, direct but not unkind. "She needs to get some sleep."

They both agree, and after a few more questions, they stand up to go, shaking both our hands.

When I go to the bathroom after they've said goodbye, a check in the mirror confirms the pain I feel. My face is a mass of purple, and while both eyelids are bright red from crying, one eyelid is swollen, a bruise covering it. The stitches in my forehead ache, and I touch them gingerly.

He knocks on the bathroom door. "Can I get you anything?"

"Pain pills?" I point at my face. "And I need to make a call." He angles his head but doesn't prod. "Let me see your face, and then you can use my cell." He admires my face in the bathroom light, his fingers on my cheek as he examines me, his light touch almost unnoticeable. He traces the bruises and kisses my forehead. "I'll be right back." He comes back holding a glass of water and some stronger Ibuprofen than the over-the-counter medication. He sets his phone on the counter.

"I'll give you a minute." I bow my head in thanks.

I dial 'o' for the operator and get the number for Maddy's house.

She picks up on the first ring. I don't even say hello before I hear sobbing into the phone.

"Levin, is that you?" She's barely audible through the tears.

"Yes, Maddy, it's me." I start to break down. "I just wanted to tell you... I'm okay."

"Thank God. I was, we were, we were both so worried." I can hear her husband murmuring in the background.

"I'm so appreciative for everything. It means so much to me." I clutch the phone in my hand, a lifeline to Maddy.

"Are you safe? Where are you?" She's full of questions, and I hear the television sound dissipate "I'm safe, and Jake is with me."

"Ahh, yes, the one who contacted me. I'm so glad he suspected you were in danger." She's breathing heavily, the events of the day a nightmare for her family as well. "You get some sleep and call me in the morning, you hear?"

"Of course," I whisper. "I can never thank you enough."

"You talking to me is enough." We both pause a moment soaking in the silence, two friends bonded over a tragedy. I hang up, too tired to concentrate. Sleep is imminent, but I'm dirty from my fall, and I feel unclean—Alec touching me and the dress still itchy even though I'm not wearing it. I shudder involuntarily thinking of the wedding.

"Bed or shower?" His voice a lullaby, careful not to startle me as I'm staring off in the distance leaning against the bathroom counter.

"I'll get the shower ready for you." He squeezes past me and reaches for the showerhead. "Or do you want a bath?"

"I want a bath, but I'll take a shower." I'm too tired to sit in the tub, plus the memory of my last bath is fresh in my mind.

He understands with a nod, as he turns on the water. "I'll shower after you."

I make a mewing sound, the idea of being alone in the shower unwanted. He angles his head, studying my face. "Do you need help?"

I'm not wearing much, my robe, and the bra and panties I had on earlier. I shake my head in response, my body quivering as he comes close to me, into my space, and tugs on the robe sash. It falls to the floor. He glides the rest of the fabric off my shoulders. His eyes are bright, too bright, the gold flecks shining.

I bite my lip. He takes his finger and touches the space I have just chewed. There's a warning sign in his eyes. I can tell he wants me, but he knows this isn't the right time.

His voice is gruff. "What do you sleep in?" He turns around so his back's to me, letting me finish undressing. "I'll grab it for you."

The water's running, but I don't get in. I'm holding onto the wall, unsure if I want even a shower curtain to separate Jake and me.

"Naked," I respond, barely audible.

"I'll get you a tee." His voice brooks no argument. He doesn't hear me move or make any effort to get in the shower. He grabs the door handle and leaves the bathroom.

I sit down on the edge of the tub examining my cut-up legs and the broken skin.

My head leans back, and I close my eyes, drifting off, the water soothing me to sleep.

There's a knock on the door a few minutes later, and I lift my head.

Jake sticks his head in. "Everything okay?"

He sees me sitting on the edge, naked, and the bathroom a steam trap, the mirrors fogged over.

I don't respond.

He enters, small steps over to me.

"Do you need me to sit in here while you shower?" He keeps his gaze locked on my face.

I swallow. "Yes, please."

He gives me a hand and helps me to stand. I put one leg over the tub and then the next. My muscles are sore, the tension lessening since I took the pills but still slowing down my movements. He closes the curtain, and I hear a thud as he sits down on the toilet seat. I lean against the wall, my hands against the tiles. I'm too exhausted to do much of anything. I use my bar soap, scrubbing the traces of the day still on me—remnants of Alec slide down the drain.

"Jake," my voice muffled over the water.

"Uh-huh."

"Just checking."

I finish up. "I'll leave the shower on for you," I offer.

"Thanks." He hands me a towel for my hair and helps me towel off my body, careful not to irritate my already punctured skin.

As I'm brushing my teeth, he peels his clothing off and gets in the shower, all in one swift movement. There's a cotton nightshirt he found that's hanging on the hook over my door. I put it on and then head to my bedroom in search of a brush for my hair.

I leave the door open to the bathroom, reassurance he's close if he's in viewing range.

When he's done taking a shower, he almost trips over me in the doorway as he comes into my bedroom.

"Let me help you to bed." He reaches a hand down to help me up.

"You're not leaving, are you?" I start to panic gripping his fingers.

"No, but I'm going to sleep on the couch."

I furiously shake my head no.

"Then the chair in here?"

"No." I'm adamant. "Will you sleep in my bed?"

His eyes widen. I can tell there's a war going on in his head, as he decides if that's the right thing to do.

"I snore." He grins.

"I drool." A small smile on my face.

He helps me to bed propping pillows up, arranging the covers over me, this place as foreign to me as a hotel room, like a stranger I've just met. I'm still amazed Jake found me in time, the whirring in my brain a snapshot of the week.

"Will you stay with me?" The drowsiness in my voice apparent, and he gets in beside me tucking me in the crook of his arm.

"Goodnight, Levin." He kisses my cheek and my forehead, his lips soft and wet, as I lean my head into the pillows.

After a few moments in his arms, my body starts to relax into his, and I start to settle, finally feeling safe. He brushes my hair back from my face, avoiding the wounded areas, and holds my hand in his anchoring me to his body.

I fall asleep almost instantaneously tethered to Jake, my body enveloped under the covers, the day's events hopefully behind me, even in my mind.

The feeling of peacefulness doesn't last, and I wake up in the middle of the night. I feel a coldness like someone rubbed an icicle down my cheek.

I touch it, the spot chilled where I felt it.

My body tenses in the dark as I figure out where I am. My

eyes are searching the darkness, spotting a pile of clothes I thought was a person.

I slacken when I realize I'm in bed with Jake.

He's snoring, the faint rise and fall of his chest matching the rhythm of his grunts, and though he's loosened his grip on me, he's still behind me, spooning me.

My muscles unwind, and I settle back into his arms.

I fall back into a deep slumber and am lucky enough that Alec doesn't haunt my dreams tonight.

Eric does, though, almost like it was his touch on my face. A reminder he's watching out for me. I miss him so much, it hurts in a way that goes beyond everything I experienced in the past seventy-two hours.

He's sitting with me in our old apartment, and we're talking about our lives, all the changes since we've been apart, and the past.

It's one of my favorite times with him—us sprawled out on the sofa, my legs laying over his lap while we watched episodes of Will & Grace or re-runs of Seinfeld.

Usually, we just laid in companionable silence or would joke around, but this time, the mood has changed.

We aren't wearing comfortable pajamas or sweats. In fact, he's wearing the suit he was buried in at his funeral, pinstriped with a high collar to hide the belt marks.

He looks over at me, and though it scares me at first, he whispers, "You saved my life."

I wake up, and I feel Eric standing in the room, his presence like a warm blanket, like the robe I can't dispose of.

I know he's there, watching over me. I smile and snuggle back down into Jake's arms.

The next morning, I awake to find Jake asleep with his mouth hanging open, catching flies, and he's managed to roll back over onto me while taking up a majority of the bed. I laugh.

I kiss his cheek and move in closer to him. His eyelids flicker open as I smirk at him.

"Jake?"

"Yes, Levin?"

"Thanks for saving my life."

"You're welcome, my miracle babe. I'm glad I decided you were worth it." He smiles at me, the mega one that stretches across his face.

He's cognizant of my bruises and traces his finger across my face. I close my eyes relaxing into his touch.

"What now?" he asks.

I don't bother opening my eyes. "I guess back to San Diego."

"Where's home for you?" I ask him.

He's been staying at the villa, but I didn't know where he even lived.

"I'm renovating a property here." Jake's leaning on his side, facing me. "Hence, the resort stay."

The idea of going back to a house that's not even my home, shared with a madman, makes my heart pound in my chest.

"Levin," Jake interrupts my thoughts. "Come stay with me. You shouldn't be alone."

I search his hazel eyes and put my hands on either side of his face. I nod in agreement.

"And really, I don't want you to go." He kisses my cheek. "You can just recuperate, figure out what you wanna do next, not have any pressure."

I nestle back into his arms and know that I'm secure. Jake's mission is mine.

There's no more running, no more trepidation about what the future holds. Alec has lost his grip on me, I'm no longer his possession.

In my mind, I thought I had known what love was, how it

existed, how you grasped it in your hand and then held onto it—a moth to a flame. In reality, Alec had taken advantage of the fact that I lost Eric. I was only ever a pawn.

Now I can stop hiding. Alec had hunted me, but Jake had found me.

CHAPTER FIFTY-SIX

ALEC

I'M SITTING IN PRISON—A 5X5 STEEL TRAP. SINCE THE crime is a little more serious than a drunk driving arrest, I'm alone.

My one call is to my attorney.

I ask him to call Mark's wife, Marian. She is, after all, an accomplice in this. My mind wanders back to the night I met her at a low-key bar after weeks of silence since our first meeting at my office. She left my office in disgust that day, my words unable to placate her. I thought she had made up her mind to ruin our business until she contacted me out of the blue asking me to meet her in a part of town neither of us would have been caught dead in. It seemed to be the type of place you would hire a hitman.

Fitting, really, due to the circumstances.

"I want him gone," Marian says this conversationally as if she's discussing fabrics or paint color swatches. "He's going to take half the

house, expect me to stay in this town, and co-parent with him. I want him gone."

I didn't know how to proceed. Was this a test? Was her phone documenting this conversation? I couldn't see the benefit in that. I hadn't wronged her. She knew I did not know of Eric's relationship with Mark before her visit to my office.

"Gone in what way?" I play dumb, unsure if she's talking about her husband or Eric.

She shoots a round of tequila, and I'm impressed by her ability to drink the potent stuff. "I want Eric gone."

"Marian," I drown my whiskey sour. "Why Eric?"

"Why not him?" Marian looks at me, a sour expression crumbling her face in the dimly-lit bar.

"With all due respect, if Mark is gay, there will be another one... even with Eric out of the picture." I tug on my ear, the intermittent ringing starting to crowd my thoughts. I can't hum in this loud honky-tonk bar.

"If Mark disappears, it looks suspect," Marian says matter-of-factly. "He's a well-known local, we have lots of money, and it's known we've had problems."

"But that money is yours, not his."

"I know." Marian sighs. "But he still gets his business and half the house. The divorce is imminent, but I want to hurt him. And he loves Eric."

I consider this for a minute. Before I can answer, she continues, "If not, I will tell my father."

I stare her down, her oversized lips in a tight line. "You will lose your clientele. Business will go under. Eric will be ruined regardless. But so will you."

The words 'uppity Pinocchio bitch' come to mind, but I let it rest on the tip of my tongue. Her father does refer a significant amount of clients to us. She's not wrong in the assumption our business will be shattered. Reputations ruined. Affairs are one thing, but Marian is ruthless in her quest to destroy both men, including me in the process.

A guard calls for another inmate down the hall. The noisy din of jail is going to prevent me from sleeping tonight. I click my fingers on the metal bench. If I'm going down for the attempted murder of Levin and the murder of Eric, Marian's coming with me.

That night she asked me to do Eric in, I was paranoid about her recording me. She should've been worried about *me* getting *her* on the record.

It's just in my nature to keep tabs on others.

My mouth moves into a wide smile. I assume I'll have a phenomenal legal team assigned to me to help get me off.

Paid for by Marian. In exchange for my undying gratitude. And silence.

A short, high-pitched laugh escapes my lips. It's imperative to have a Plan B.

ABOUT MARIN MONTGOMERY

Marin Montgomery is a thirty-something Phoenician transplant with champagne taste and the bluest eyes you'll ever see. When she's not jet setting across the continent for her job in corporate America, you can find her soaking up the sun and dreaming up her next masterpiece.

Feel free to drop her a line at: authormarin@gmail.com

Follow her on Facebook: https://www.facebook.com/authormarinmontgomery/

or join her private mailing list here: http://eepurl.com/c7NQjL

71186440R00156

Made in the USA
Middletown, DE
20 April 2018